PIOUS

a novel

PIOUS

a novel

KENN BIVINS

Two Harbors Press
212 3rd Avenue North, Suite 290
Minneapolis, MN 55401
612.455.2293
www.TwoHarborsPress.com

ISBN - 978-1-936198-66-5
ISBN - 1-936198-66-5
LCCN - 2010934066

Illustration by Kenn Bivins
Typeset by James Arneson

Printed in the United States of America

For Kenn II and Spencer. All that I do is for you.

No man for any considerable period can wear one face to himself and another to the multitude, without finally getting bewildered as to which may be the true.

—Nathaniel Hawthorne, *The Scarlet Letter*

CHAPTER ONE

Carpious Mightson is not who he appears to be while portraying all that he isn't. The appearance of friendliness and virtue suits him comfortably as he moves about his yard one Saturday morning, raking leaves as the autumn breeze lulls the branches above him.

Carpious, looming wide-shouldered at six foot two inches, is not much different from the three towering and massive trees that dominate his lawn as he gathers leaves into modest piles at the end of his yard. His two-hundred-twenty-pound frame is dressed with blue, baggy sweat pants and a black jersey while his yellowish-brown skin gives off a glow that is much like the leaves that are all about him. His close-cropped salt and pepper hair is exposed to a cool autumn breeze as he, like every Saturday for the past month, busies himself in his yard, a chore that allows him a semblance of a social outing where he can spend time talking with his neighbors.

"Why don't you just use a leaf blower?" says a voice from behind Carpious. He'd had his back to the street and was looking toward his house at the work he'd done thus far. His thoughts were distant enough from his surroundings to be startled by the sudden voice.

Carpious sharply turns to see a short, older man shuffling toward him with a limp and warm smile. Bernie Loomis is a sixty-three-year old widower and neighbor from across the street that grew fond of Carpious almost immediately when they met two years ago. Bernie's New Jersey accent, balding head, and thick black eyebrows liken him to a caricature found in the editorial section of a Sunday newspaper. He's wearing a gray pullover, the signature piece to every ensemble he wears. His arms swing back and forth as a toy wind-up soldier's might as he walks toward Carpious.

Carpious' heavy brows are raised as a subtle smile spreads across his face. "I'm sorry. What was that?"

"A leaf blower." Bernie pants like the walk across the street exhausted him. "Why don't you use…one of those to help you? You won't have to…work so hard."

Carpious, with a full smile on his face now, reaches his hand out to steady Bernie and greet his portly and out-of-breath neighbor. An expensive platinum watch on Bernie's outstretched arm peeks out from under the ragged sleeve of his gray pullover betraying the otherwise Bohemian appearance.

"You okay, Bern? Do you wanna take a seat on the porch?"

"Nah, I'm fine." He exhales deeply. "My meds got changed last week and I've been out of sorts ever since. Nothing a little exercise won't hurt, right? Maybe I should do like you and rake my own leaves."

Carpious politely chuckles. "I don't use a leaf blower 'cause I'm old school." He reaches down and grabs a handful of leaves and crushes them in his hand. "I love the crisp, crackling sound of the leaves as I drag them across the lawn. Hear that? A motor would just drown that beautiful sound out and wake half the neighborhood. I'm sure my resting neighbors wouldn't think so well of me then, eh?"

Bernie reaches down with one hand on his knee to balance himself and grabs a small handful of leaves with his other hand. He straightens himself and holds up his handful of leaves, crushing them.

"You hear that?" he asks Carpious with a controlled smile on his face. "That is the sound my sixty-three-year-old back would be making if I tried raking these leaves without a blower."

Bernie barely finishes his sentence before he bursts out into laughter. His eyes crinkle and his pale, splotchy face turns beet red as he leans against Carpious' arm swinging his other hand uncontrollably at the hilarity. Carpious again politely echoes his laugh, waiting for a cue to fade his reserved chuckle.

That attentiveness and patience are two of the qualities that endear Carpious to Bernie, who has been suffering bouts of loneliness since the sudden death of his wife three years ago. She was his high school sweetheart, and they had been married forty-four years before an aggressive brain tumor caused a sudden and fatal aneurysm. The introduction of Carpious a year later was an answer to Bernie's prayer for a friend—a "patient, God-fearing, respectful good listener."

Bernie's laughter tapers off and he reaches into his back pocket. "Oh, wait. Before I forget why I came over…I got some of your mail again. I don't want you accusing me of cashing your million dollar checks."

Carpious laughs a more natural laugh this time,

reaching for the plain, white envelope as he looks at Bernie, saying, "If you find any million dollar checks with my name on them, I'll split the winnings fifty-fifty."

Bernie chuckles, "Deal!"

Carpious looks down in the midst of laughing and glances at the official print on the envelope. His grin slips away so quickly that it snags Bernie's.

"I didn't recognize it as your mail at first, but then I saw the last name and your address. Is that your sister or something?"

"Or something." Carpious quickly looks up while attempting to recover his previous jovial expression. "My ex-wife."

"Ex-wife? Really? I didn't know you were ever married."

"Yeah. It was a long time ago. A lifetime ago. This must be insurance information. You know how slow they are about removing names from documents and whatnot. Thanks, Bernie."

"You're welcome. You'll have to tell me about that past life of yours someday over a glass of Scotch," Bernie teases.

Carpious laughs more. "Past life? I'm sure my past life is a boring bedtime story to you. There's not a whole lot there to tell."

They both laugh.

Bernie points his chin up the street asking, "Did you notice the FOR SALE sign at 361 went down a couple days ago?"

As he leans on the handle of his rake, Carpious' eyes follow Bernie's gesture, "No, I didn't notice, but there's been a sign in front of that house for close to a year. It's about time someone bought it."

"Yeah, it'll be good to have our neighborhood back. It seemed like the agent who was showing the house would bring people through at the oddest hours. I wonder if it's another family."

The family-friendly neighborhood of Mechi Lane is populated with houses of varying styles that were constructed during different building trends over the past thirty years. A peppering of stucco, vinyl, and brick are a testament to the neighborhood's diversity. The cars that line the manicured driveways further attest that this is a neighborhood of varying demographics. Whole and carved pumpkins planted on many of the porches hint that Halloween is near. Deflated yard skeletons, witches, and other ghoulish cartoon characters testify that it has already passed.

Carpious' house, 163 Mechi Lane, is the second one on the left side of the subdivision's entrance. Both the dense oak trees and the brick exterior of his home suggest that his house was one of the first to be established in the neighborhood. The houses further up the street lining the cul-de-sac are newer, more cost-efficient structures and only have newly planted saplings to complement the front yards articulated by manicured sod tracts.

"That would be nice. Never can have too many kids arou—"

Bernie interrupts himself, looking past Carpious, and gleams a smile much brighter than his previous ones. Carpious turns his head to discover what has gained Bernie's attention.

Haleigh Janson's high-pitched, seven-year-old voice

asks, "Can I help you, Mr. Mightson?"

"Hello there, young lady," Bernie beams.

Haleigh glances at Bernie but barely acknowledges him. Her blue eyes, framed with freckles and dark, short hair are fixated on the several piles of leaves and what Carpious' response will be.

She repeats, "Can I help you with the leaves, Mr. Mightson? I'm a good helper."

Much like a calm, yet stern parent, Carpious says, "Haleigh, Mr. Loomis said hello to you. Aren't you going to be polite and say hello back?"

"Hi, Mr. Loooomusis," Haleigh whines.

Bernie's body shakes as he quietly chuckles and turns to Carpious.

Pointing at the pile of leaves, Carpious smiles, "I'll tell you what…why don't you rake those three little piles into one *big* pile? You can use my rake and I'll go get my other one. Okay?"

"Okay!"

"And if you do a good job, we'll see if it's okay with your mom and dad if you can have a snack."

Carpious looks toward the house next door and sees Haleigh's mom sitting in a swing on the porch. He waves.

"Good morning, Lela."

Waving back, she says, "Good morning, Carpious. I hope she's not bothering you."

"*Bothering* me? This is my partner in crime. She's okay."

"Okay."

He pats Bernie on the shoulder and smiles as he turns to walk toward his garage.

"Be right back."

Bernie returns the smile and nods his head. "Take

your time, Carpious. I'll just hang out here."

~

Lela Janson is entering the fifth month of her preg-nancy. Aside from frequent trips to the bathroom and not being able to sleep comfortably, she is progressing quite well. As she sits on the porch swing with several pillows about her, she studies her firstborn in the yard next door as she struggles to handle a garden tool twice her size. It was only seven years ago that she carried Haleigh in her belly. That pregnancy was much different though. She almost miscarried in the first trimester and was put on bed rest for the rest of her pregnancy.

She smiles at the thought of the miracle of Haleigh, a smile so big that it puffs her freckled cheeks out and almost closes her eyes. Aside from a protruding belly and a comical waddle when she walks, her body fails to show signs of age. In appearance, she is the adult and pregnant version of her daughter.

The front door to 175 Mechi Lane swings open.

"Haleigh? Haleigh!"

"She's next door, Drew," Lela answers her husband as she shifts around slightly to see him.

"Oh. She was supposed to be helping me clean up the kitchen. Do you need anything else?"

He closes the door and hands Lela a mug that has steam rising from it. She looks up at him and smiles.

"No. This hot chocolate is a most excellent comple-ment to a perfect breakfast. Thank you, honey."

Drew moves a couple of pillows out of the way to make room and sits next to Lela. "You're welcome. Are you sure it's okay to drink that, love? The doctor said that caffei—"

Lela whines, "Honey, I've been good. No coffee, no wine, no chocolate. I've earned this one cup." Lela sips. "Mmmmm. Thank you again for a great morning, honey. I know I've been a handful the past few months and I know you're trying. I just want you to know that I applaud your patience."

Lela smiles to herself before continuing, "I love our life. I'm...happy."

Drew rubs Lela's back and seems to strain a smile as he sits back to observe the early morning activity humming around him. His temporary smile fades as he stares off into the distance at no certain thing. His mind is clearly not on the wife beside him or the daughter clumsily raking leaves with their neighbor.

What makes people happy? Is it the release of endorphins by the pituitary gland? Is it a surface place of comfort brought on by external conveniences? Or is it simply a cerebral choice? Drew ponders and listens to the silence for a moment.

"Why do you say that?" he asks Lela in an unfeeling voice as he continues to stare ahead.

"What?" she asks.

His eyes are still fixed straight ahead. "You say that you love our life. Why do you say that?"

"Honey, I say it because I mean it. We have a good life. I mean, I know things could be worse and we've come a long way."

Drew breaks his stare and turns to face Lela. His eyes say a million confusing things before his lips are bold enough to use words.

"Lela... I—I'm *not* so happy," Drew confesses as he

slowly shakes his head.

Lela returns an expression of concern and betrayal. The mug that she was previously holding close to her face while letting the steam warm her is lowered to her lap.

"What do you mean? How can you say that? What's wrong?"

Drew looks away and his jaw tightens as if he's stubbornly holding back some sort of confession. Tense seconds pass in silence.

"Our life is so…routine. We're parents and that's all we are. Everything we do is about Haleigh or the baby. I thought having another baby would bring us closer, but I feel like we're in two different realities. You're happy and content, and I see that the emperor isn't wearing any clothes."

Tears well up in Lela's eyes as she looks away, her chin quivering.

"Lela, I love you, and you know it, but…"

Lela sharply turns to face Drew with a stony expression on her face. The tears that were coming forth have been ordered back.

Drew continues, "I don't know if I can do this. I don't want our kids to grow up, leave the house, and leave you and I as strangers to one another."

"And I don't…!"

Lela pauses to compose herself.

She continues, "I don't want our kids to grow up with a father who wants to be anywhere else but here!" she exclaims.

They both retreat to a sudden silence as they simultaneously look around, realizing that they are on the porch of their home in plain view and earshot of their neighbors. But no one seems disturbed by Lela's outburst.

Lela leans toward Drew with a stern whisper, "I thought you got past this! We've had this discussion before, and you said that you were just going through some stuff in your head. We both decided to have this baby! After counseling and your recommitment to our marriage, I trusted you. What is this crap now?"

"This is reality, Lela. I've been trying hard to—"

"So what was this morning? Breakfast? Kind words? Cleaning up? What the heck is that? To butter me up so you could tell me that our marriage isn't as great as I've been led to believe?"

Lela doesn't wait for a response as she jerks up. She flings her arm toward the shrubbery in front of the porch emptying the remaining contents of her mug. She abruptly turns, avoiding further eye contact with Drew, and swings the door open to go inside. The door slams shut.

Drew shyly looks up and sees that Haleigh is looking in his direction, but she immediately resumes her labor of swinging the rake through the piles of leaves.

"That went well," Drew sarcastically whispers to himself.

~

Deidre Merritt sits outside a busy café where the regulars occupy a smattering of seats inside. The café is neither a corporate franchise nor a shameful attempt at duplicating such. The writing on the window simply reads, "CAFÉ." The glass door is cluttered with flyers advertising upcoming open mic nights, past music festivals, handyman services, and lost dogs. Outside are three sets of lightweight iron tables and rickety chairs—one of which Deidre occupies.

She combs her fingers through her locks to draw them from her face as she looks at her watch for a second time. She is very early for an appointment with a client. A stranger would guess from her appearance that she has a client somewhere who was just sold an insurance policy, an expensive piece of equipment, or a parcel of real estate.

The wind is gusty and leaves scurry across the pavement mimicking the sound of distant applause. Seated at the table to the right of where she's facing are two men in their thirties. They seem very intimate based on how close at which they sit to one another. Speaking in French, both men wear glasses and are in advanced stages of balding. One wears a gray T-shirt and white shorts while the other is dressed more seasonably in a black knit sweater and blue jeans. Deidre can't help but hear their raised voices and assume from the tone that they are discussing something they are both passionate and angry about.

Seated at the table to her left and behind her is a woman who sounds as though she is in her late fifties. She's speaking loudly into her cell phone to someone she seems to be counseling through a crisis. The woman mentions the situation being in God's hands several times and apparently is more impressed with the sound of her own voice than that of the person on the other end of the call.

Cars whiz by the café with less frequency than the

busy leaves that scurry across the sidewalk. An early model, blue BMW sedan slows as it passes to turn into a parking lot on the side of the building. Deidre is roused from her people watching to see the vehicle disappear around the corner.

A few seconds pass before a man appears from behind the corner where his car disappeared. He walks with a meek confidence and is what some might describe as boyishly handsome. He's wearing textured, gray slacks and a light blue button-down shirt that is covered with a tan blazer. His black penny loafers and gel-sculpted hair scream "trust-fund-kid" or at least "preppy." He appears to be in his early thirties. As he gets nearer to her table, Deidre, who has made eye contact with him, stands to greet him with a smile.

"Hello, Mr. Kaplan. Good to see you," she says as she firmly shakes his hand.

He returns apologetically, "Hi, Ms. Merritt. I'm sorry if I'm a few minutes late. I got totally turned around after I took the wrong exit. I'm not too familiar with this area." He pulls out a chair and sits.

"Oh it's okay. I got here early and you're right on time. This'll be your neighborhood soon, so what better time to get acquainted, huh? We could've met at the house but there's no heat or electricity on right now. It's probably freezing there. I figure here we can score a cup of coffee while you sign these last few papers, Mr. Kaplan."

"Uh...I know you're being professional but, we're practically the same age. Ian is okay."

"Okay, Ian. Would you like some coffee or tea?"

"No, thank you. I'm good."

Deidre reaches into a slim attaché case that was

sitting beside her chair and pulls out a small stack of documents that have colorful Post-it notes strategically placed on each page. She hands him the documents that are bound together by a paperclip.

"Since you're applying through a government program for your loan, there are a few more papers that you need to sign. Your loan is already in process, but I'm sure they'll ask for these documents at some point. It's best that we be proactive and submit them now so that you can close before the end of November. We wouldn't want red tape slowing anything down. "

She hands Ian a pen but he holds his own up.

"As you can see, I've flagged the places where I'll need you to sign. The documents are self-explanatory, but I can answer any questions that you may have."

"Thanks," Ian says as he begins to study the documents with his pen leading his eyes. He scribbles his signature at the appointed places as he scans each page. Suddenly, he squints with the pen pointing at the origin of his concern.

"My name is misspelled with an 'm' instead of an 'n' and...um...the address is wrong. It says 362 Mechi Lane but it should be *361*."

Deidre leans in focusing on the paper and instructs, "Okay. Draw a line though the errors, write the correct information above it, and then initial it. That should be good. I'm sorry about the typos." Deidre sits back. "You said you had some more questions for me."

Ian's attention is drawn from Deidre as he silently mouths words while running his fingers across the papers before signing them. He signs the final sheet and looks up gathering the papers together again.

"Yeah. I wanted to know if there were any problems with my application and all that I disclosed. I don't want anything coming up at the last minute."

Deidre seems puzzled for a second and then recalls what Ian may be referring to. Almost immediately, her perplexed expression turns to compassion.

"Mr. Kap...er...Ian, you told me about your previous conviction before you registered a serious interest in buying property at Mechi Lane. As I told you then, you are well within your legal rights."

"I know that you talked to your legal team and checked the state and county statutes, but I just want to make sure that I don't run into problems here. This isn't some rental property. This will be my *home*."

"Mr. Kaplan, your records show that you've settled your debt to society and completed the proper counseling hours to deem you fit to live at Mechi Lane."

Ian's voice crackles, "I know that. You have access to my records, so you know that. But my new neighbors—who may be curious about me and find out that I'm a registered sex offender—will not know that."

"Ian, I'm your real estate agent, not your probation officer, your caseworker, or your therapist. I can't advise you professionally nor can I imagine what you're going through emotionally. But I do know that since you've served your debt to society, your past is your past."

Ian's boyish looks coupled with the concern in his eyes reduce his reaction to the mannerisms of a scared twelve-year-old. He lived in an apartment complex previous to now. The fact that he stayed off of the radar of any vigilant neighbors gave him the boldness to look at purchasing a home and starting his life over.

A little over one year ago, he was released from prison after serving eleven years for statutory rape. Eleven years for not knowing that a twenty-year-old woman he had sex with was in fact a thirteen-year-old girl. Eleven years for not being astute enough to know the difference. Eleven years punishment for spending too much time on high school campuses long after he'd graduated from high school. Eleven years for being "sick." Eleven years to now be labeled a sex offender.

Ian shyly responds, "Yeah, I guess you're right. I'm just nervous. You hear stories about people making assumptions and doing crazy things, you know."

"As I've already said, you are well within your legal rights to live in this house."

Saying nothing, Ian stares back.

"Ian, as I've said, I'm not your probation officer nor am I your therapist, but if I may be so bold…it's admirable that you're moving forward with your life. I applaud you. Don't be afraid. *You* determine who you will be. *You* define who you want people to see. *You* are the sum total of your past, but that past does not have to become you. This move will be a good thing for you. You'll see."

Ian smiles and looks around nervously. He seems suddenly conscious of anyone who may be listening to their conversation.

CHAPTER TWO

Sunlight traces the brick edifice of Admah City Community Church, granting it a prominent presence as dozens of people file into the building for Sunday morning service. The façade of the building boasts four giant white pillars equally spaced that draw subconscious comparisons to the architecture of early Rome. The pillars that reach toward the clear, fall sky are capped with decorative capitals, featuring carved figures of some presumed importance. A casual theologian or historian might be able to interpret that the figures symbolize some period of church history. Ironically perched atop the massive building is a humble steeple and cross that forgive the less-than-conventional characteristics.

Below, dozens of people of different ages and cultures climb the brick stairway that divides the great pillars. If the dress of the people filing through the oversized brown doors is any indication of the tone of worship service, one would be inclined to assume that this church is of a contemporary nature. Inside, the 750-seat auditorium confirms that assumption. The rows of seats lead to a grand stage that is dimly lit and casts shadows on several configurations of musical equipment. On either side of the stage are immense projector screens that look like LCDs showing colorful advertisements and announcements for various available ministries. Outside, tall, narrow windows on the sides of the building give further evidence that this is a modern congregation. Dark and tinted glass framed in white adorns this place of worship where images of saints in stained glass would otherwise be.

The expansive parking lot on the left side of the building is crowded with cars of varying makes and models. Though the lot seems to be full to capacity, two off-duty sheriff's deputies direct more incoming traffic there. A white, twelve-foot, framed sign in front of the church serves to inform oncoming traffic that this is indeed a place of worship, as if the cross atop the building were not hint enough. The calligraphic letters that are stylish though legible from the street read, "Admah City Community Church." Beneath the name, smaller plain text reads, "Russell Moser, Senior Pastor."

~

Carpious unfolds from his silver 2004 Honda Accord like a moth from its cocoon. The length of his drive to the church was far longer than he remembered it being last week. Perhaps long hours of work coupled with Sunday traffic had begun to take their toll on him. He straightens his jacket by sharply shrugging his shoulders a few times and then irons his shirt with his hands while tucking in any excess cloth that fails to comply with his degree of neatness. Though his hair is too short to be mussed, he wipes his hairline and face of any oil that would give his amber skin an uneven shine. He closes the car door and before he can turn to join the exodus from the parking into the massive building, he sees in a reflection in his door window.

"Sydney! Good morning," Carpious turns to greet the woman approaching.

Sydney Durden is a statuesque, dark-skinned woman who stands five foot seven without the stilettos she's wearing. Her stately presence is further marked by medium brown, curly hair that is styled with a part down the middle that draws attention to her light brown gaze and porcelain-smooth face. Her smile exposes perfectly straight and bright teeth, complemented by dimples on either side of her cheeks. Walking alongside her and holding her slender hand is a little boy whose stature is much more humble and withdrawn. He looks to be about eight years old, and his chubby appearance, framed with T-shirt, jeans, and an unkempt curly afro, indicates he is content with simply being a little boy and nothing more.

Sydney enthusiastically answers, "Carpious! I thought you were going to be out of town this weekend."

"Me too, but the trip got cancelled at the last minute because the audit isn't happening. Something about a settlement, but I'm not complaining. I could use the break from traveling for a few weeks anyway. It's good to break the monotony of the office once in a while, but not every week."

"I know. I was beginning to forget what you look like," Sydney flirts as she stretches her free hand out to touch Carpious on the arm.

Carpious responds by pulling Sydney close and engulfing her in a hug. She returns the sentiment with much elation. As the reunion that appears to be much more than platonic concludes, Carpious looks around at the little boy by Sydney's side who is now hiding behind her waist.

"Hey, Solo! High five."

Carpious raises his arm just above the little boy's head with his palm facing him.

Solomon Durden springs from behind his mother to participate in a greeting that he and Carpious have shared for six months now. He meets Carpious' palm with a loud smack.

Then Carpious lowers his hand to Solomon's level, "Low five!"

Solomon again meets the demand with a smack.

"Down low."

Carpious holds his hand out lower this time and right before Solomon connects with his hand, he snatches it away and scoops Solomon up in a hug.

"Too slow!"

Solomon gleefully giggles and screams before Carpious releases him. They all walk toward the church building together.

"What are you doing this evening? Have you made any other plans since I was supposed to be out of town?" Carpious asks, returning his attention toward Sydney.

"I promised Solomon that I would let him play at the park this afternoon after church and then I have to cook dinner. It's a typical Sunday. After that, we have no plans. Why?"

Solomon looks up at Carpious and his mom, fixated on what they may be conspiring to do.

Aware that he has an audience, Carpious leans in close to Sydney and whispers, "Why don't you skip the park and let me cook dinner for you guys? I'm sure there'll be kids for Solomon to play with, and he loves it there."

Sydney giggles much like an infatuated schoolgirl and teases, "You had me at 'let me cook you dinner.'"

Carpious laughs. Solomon smiles quietly at what he has overheard. Either he has extremely acute hearing or Carpious is not very good at whispering.

As the makeshift trio navigates through the sea of people who have converged at the giant doors of the church, the smile of a short, portly woman wearing a brightly colored dress and scarf greets them.

"Carpious! Sydney! Solomon! Good morning. This is the day that the Lord has made. Are you all rejoicing?"

"Yes, ma'am," Carpious returns with perfect timing and a wide smile. "How are *you* doing this morning? I *love* that dress. You're wearing my favorite colors—brown, orange, and yellow with a *splash* of green. Go on 'head, Mrs. Leonard."

Mrs. Leonard blushes, and though she is at least twenty years older than Carpious, she giggles like a teenage girl.

Sydney joins in with, "You *do* look beautiful, Mrs. Leonard."

Mrs. Leonard mimics a curtsey and smiles, "Thank you. Thank you. You all are too kind. Such a beautiful couple and look at this handsome young man."

She bends down slightly and gently squeezes Solomon's cheeks as he shyly nudges toward his mother's waist.

"Carpious, I just want to say thank you for that book that you dropped by my office last week. I wish I'd caught you before you left."

"Oh, it's my pleasure. I was on your side of town and figured that you could use the encouragement."

Sydney looks at Carpious with a sense of pride, not sure of what the two are speaking of as the crowd nudges them forward.

"Well, let me let you fine people go on into the service. You all be encouraged."

"Be blessed," Carpious recites as Mrs. Leonard is suddenly distracted by another cluster of people a few feet away.

"What was that about?" Sydney inquires as she leans into Carpious.

Before he can answer, a voice from behind Carpious asks, "Brother Mightson, how's the Lord been treating you?"

Carpious turns around at the touch of a hand on his right shoulder, though he has not heard what has been asked of him. He looks down and sees a short man wearing a tweed jacket with khaki pants and a white shirt complemented by an impressively creative comb-over and glasses smiling up at him.

"Oh hey, Roy," Carpious replies.

"How's the good Lord been treating you?" Roy repeats, smiling in an almost plastic and forced manner.

"Oh, I can't complain. The Lord is in the business of blessing, and I just keep getting in his business."

Roy's laugh is almost as counterfeit as his smile.

Roy continues, "Hey, I was wondering if I could schedule some time with you in the middle of the week to go over some numbers. My business partner and I are reviewing all of our liabilities to see if we can move on a potential prospect. I know you're the expert at that sort of thing and—"

Carpious interrupts with the gesture of putting his hand on Roy's shoulder in a reassuring way.

"Just give me a call on Tuesday and we'll set something up, okay?"

"I appreciate it. Will do. Be blessed," Roy says as he disappears into the crowd.

Carpious turns to Sydney and they exchange glances and smirks in a silent exchange. Sydney chuckles quietly.

As they pass through the entryway of the sanctuary, a man who is either an usher or a greeter smiles good morning to Carpious and Sydney while handing them a program guide for the order of the service. He holds on to the paper as Carpious takes it and asks, "Hey, C, have you talked to Brian, Marc, or Todd?"

Carpious appears confused by the question and responds, "Uh…no."

"We're trying to coordinate next year's retreat and were wondering if you would be willing to host a planning meeting at your place. People listen to you and you have a way with calling everyone to action and responsibility. If *you* cosign, I'm pretty sure that others will more likely be drawn out to participate and we'll have the potential to do much better than last year."

Carpious recovers as a wave of understanding and recall has apparently come over him and he smiles.

"Oh, okay…sure. Last year *was* good, but if we'd had more people it would have been awesome."

"Exactly."

"Let me talk to Marc this week so he can catch me up to where the planning already is. We'll set something up, and you are more than welcome to use my place."

"Good, good. Thank you, C. You all enjoy the service." He pats Carpious on the shoulder and nods at Sydney as he releases the program to Carpious' grasp.

Carpious, Sydney, and Solomon make their way to seats near the middle of the auditorium.

Sydney smiles, looking at Carpious.

"C? And here I was wasting syllables calling you Carpious. You're just Mr. Popular this morning. Everyone's loving you."

Carpious looks at her smiling.

~

Pastor Russell Moser takes center stage to the attention of the congregation of Admah City Community Church. For fifteen years, he has served as pastor, counselor, administrator, servant, and friend to thousands of parishioners. Those who have known him for the length of fifteen years or for fifteen minutes would find it hard to see him in any other role, as he seems to have a natural and intense desire to help people. It is because of that very passion that Admah City Community Church has become a cornerstone in the populace of Admah City through community outreach, health fairs, scholarships for underprivileged students, substance abuse and marital counseling, and general ministry work.

Whereas many people see church or religion as a self-serving entity or business, Pastor Russell has tirelessly made it his goal to debunk that myth by unconditionally serving others with the hope that his example will influence them into a practical and personal relationship with God.

At forty-eight years old, Pastor Russell is reminiscent of a flannel-clad grandfather that smells of patchouli and hickory wood and has countless stories to tell. Most people tend to appear more or less approachable based on the clothing they wear or the hairstyle they display, but Pastor Russell looks friendly and approachable whether he's in a fine tailored suit or T-shirt and jeans. He typically shies away from wearing traditional garments or a suit during Sunday service though. He's remarked several times to those who would like to see him look "more religious" that it distances him from those whom he desires to reach—those who wander into the church out of curiosity.

Pastor Moser concludes his sermon as he walks about the podium from where he has been addressing the congregation for the past twenty minutes. Rather than using music or an excitable tone of voice to punctuate emotion, he simply talks to his congregation.

"...instead, let us be vessels of justice without judgment, love without leaving, and grace all-seeing. Let those who see us and would call us hypocrites because we carry the label of 'Christian' be humbled by our righteous living. Songs are good for praising God, but if your heart is unchanged, you're simply babbling noise like an incoherent child."

The audience is a quiet mix of respect, sleepiness, and note-taking. Carpious listens intently without blinking as does Sydney who is sitting beside him. Solomon has fallen asleep in his mother's lap as she strokes his hair.

"Who are you? Brother? Father? Mother…sister… son…daughter? When you look in the mirror, when no one is around, who are you? Who does God see? Are your actions driven by what others see or by who you *really* are?"

Carpious looks down and away as if absorbing and processing what Pastor Russell is saying. He then glances at Sydney to see if she is likewise convicted in any way. She continues to look ahead, listening intently but stopping on occasion to jot down notes in a notebook that is on top of a bible that sits open in her lap.

"My family, I challenge you to do two things this week, starting now. One: Look in the mirror of your soul and ask God to show you who you really are. Do away with the noise and the obligations of the day and listen. You can't love others without loving yourself. Two: Tell someone you love that you love them without using the word *love*."

Laughter fills the auditorium and fades back to silence almost as quickly. Sydney looks at Carpious this time, but he's looking straight ahead.

"Now, there's nothing inherently wrong with using the word *love*, but we often times simply use the word as a crutch and we never *demonstrate* love as a result. So tell someone you love them through action. Now go in peace. Amen."

Silence suddenly expires with the noise of movement and discussion. Sydney tries to wake Solomon, but he is as unresponsive and as lifeless as a giant bag of potatoes. Carpious lifts him across his chest and shoulder as if Solomon is a toddler and they make their way out of the sanctuary and to the parking lot with the rest of the crowd.

Approximately an hour and a half ago, the congregation was lazily milling about in the parking lot and lobby, talking amongst themselves. Now, conversation and small talk give way to more deliberate and continual movement to the parking lot. There are a few stragglers who stand around to discuss everything from thoughts on the message they've just heard to where to go for lunch, but they are in the minority.

Pastor Russell finds his way into the crowd of exiting people, shaking hands, exchanging hugs, and thanking people for coming. He makes eye contact with Carpious and waves. Carpious enthusiastically waves back but is too far away to exchange words.

He mouths the words, "I'll give you a call" and Pastor Russell waves again and nods in understanding.

He and Sydney walk in comfortable silence to her car. She unlocks the door to the SUV, and he eases Solomon off of his shoulder and into the backseat and buckles him in. Solomon awakens momentarily in the process.

"See you soon, Solo," Carpious says to Solomon.

Solomon sleepily nods his head as Carpious closes the door.

"So I'll see you two in a couple of hours?" he asks.

Sydney answers, "Sure. We're going home to change and relax for a bit. That'll give you time to start your magic…unless you need my help."

"No, no, no. I invited you. Guests do nothing but show up and eat."

Carpious leans in to kiss Sydney on the cheek as he hugs her, but she turns toward him and he grazes the side of her lips. He closes the door as Sydney gets in the car and waves, smiling.

"See you soon."

"Bye, sweetie."

As she pulls away, Carpious turns to walk to his own car, which is only a few feet away. A smile is affixed to his guise as he waves at a few more people. He folds into his car and turns the key in the ignition. Something draws his attention to the rearview mirror that causes him to abandon his smile. His reflection.

CHAPTER THREE

The smell of garlic wafts through the house as Carpious Mightson prepares dinner for his anticipated guests. He maneuvers about his kitchen with the skill and precision of a gourmet chef performing before a studio audience on some top-rated television cooking show. The name brand appliances and tools that adorn the kitchen bespeak a sense of quality and status that most people never see beyond cable TV or a department store showroom. Evident from such an investment, Carpious loves cooking, but none of this would be possible outside of the quality of living that being a successful auditor provides.

Eight years ago, Ardent Investments took on an inexperienced, thirty-seven-year-old Carpious on the glowing referral of respected Pastor Russell Moser. In a relatively short time, he grew from the entry-level position of Junior Financial Planner to Senior Auditor, serving some of the company's most coveted clients. His job essentially consists of looking at clients' business structures—their products, services, inventory and any related assets, debts, and other liabilities—and assessing potential loss and how best to build capital from that point within an aggressive timeframe. It's a high-risk and potentially stressful job that demands a lot of traveling, but Carpious doesn't allow the potential stresses to affect him negatively. He finds calm in the chaos of it all.

In the background, to accompany the ambience of home, is Miles Davis' album *Kind of Blue*. Previous to that was an assortment of tracks by Nina Simone, John Coltrane, and Ella Fitzgerald with the occasional religious hymn to break the routine of jazzCarpious whispers the menu of the meal that he has just prepared as he lays out the settings in the dining room.

"Salmon risotto topped with capers, steamed green beans topped with a lemon-garlic butter sauce, and red skin mashed potatoes. A top-shelf Riesling for the adults. A freshly blended strawberry, mango, and pineapple smoothie for Solomon. Optional desert choices of tiramisu or strawberry shortcake with whipped topping."

Carpious stands back to admire the setting of the table and, though the plates and the seats are empty right now, he imagines exchanging pleasantries with his guests soon.

"Sydney and Solomon should be here any mome—"

Carpious' thoughts are interrupted as he glances through the sheer curtains of the window in the dining room. He barely makes out the outline of a car that is too small to be Sydney's slowly pulling into the driveway. He pulls the curtains back slightly to reveal a blue Honda Civic from eighty-something and a familiar woman getting out.

He lets the curtains fall back to their previous state and, in a calm yet terse tone, with his jaw clenched, he mouths, "Shit!"

~

The front door swings open before the woman-visitor-who-is-not-Sydney can ring the doorbell. The expression on Carpious' face is far from agreeable as he looms in front of a woman wrapped in a quilted jacket standing five foot three inches with medium brown skin. Black, straightened and dull hair peeks out from under the thick knit hat that covers her head. The puffy jacket, oversized jeans, and suede boots do little to distract from the fact that she is a smallish woman. She wrings her gloved hands as if she is still cold and smiles.

"What the *fuck* are you doing here?" Carpious greets with a snarl.

"Nice to see you too, Carpious," she returns still smiling a smile with teeth that testify to the fact that she is or recently was a smoker.

She continues as her head and neck begin to sway in rhythm to her words, "Your neighbor, Bennie? Bumpie? Whateva. That man 'cross the street was nice enough to help me find you. You know none of these houses got numbers on 'em? How yo' mailman find y'all?"

"Alethea, what do you want?" Carpious asks calmly and deliberately with his eyes closed as if he's meditating while speaking.

"Damnnnn! I haven't seen you in five years and I get no hello, how do you do, or nothing?"

Carpious breathes, "I have no business with you now, Alethea. We are divorced. You have no reason to look for me, call me, or visit unannounced. Please leave."

Carpious steps back and begins to close the door when Alethea blurts out in a rushed and desperate manner, "I'm dying, Carpious! I got the bug. I got AIDS."

Carpious stops closing the door and answers in surprise, "What?"

The smile on Alethea's face is replaced with a hardened frown. "You heard me, motherfucka. I got AIDS. I'm gonna die and it's yo' fault." Her voice quivers, though defiant.

Carpious opens the door, looking down at Alethea and through her at the same time. An eternity of a pause passes before he says anything. "Come...come in," he stutters, blinking, his eyes frowning.

Alethea steps inside, walking past Carpious with a swagger and confidence that her announcement has thrown him off. He closes the door and turns to face her, not inviting her all the way inside.

He asks calmly while still frowning, "What are you talking about?"

Alethea turns to face Carpious and her voice continues with a quiver. "Seven years ago, when you left, I was still going through my shit. You remember? You told me I was...toxic. That's why you left, you said. You abandoned me, motherfucka! When I needed someone—my husband—to stand by me, you left me. I needed someone. So I found someone. I was desperate. I thought he loved me. He gave me the bug—no good, cheating, drug-usin' motherfucka."

Carpious laments, "Alethea, I'm sorr—"

Alethea once again recovers from her seeming emotional weakness to interrupt. "Sorry? Too late now, motherfucka!"

Her arms join the expressive chorus that her head and neck have already begun.

"I see you doing good for yo'self though. I see you done come a long way from being locked up and being one of them down-on-yo-luck Christian folk. House smelling all good and shit. Sorry? Motherfucka, please. You know how expensive my medicine is? I can't come up like you. I'm 'bout to die. And why? Cause a motherfucka can't stand by his bitch!"

Carpious exclaims while leaning toward Alethea with his right fist and finger pointing at the floor, "That's enough! You will respect me and my house! I'm sorry that you're sick but that has nothing to do with me."

"Yeah it does, motherfucka! I wouldn't be in this shit if you hadn't left me."

"You wouldn't be in your *mess* if you weren't an *addict*! Don't blame your problems on me. And why am I getting your mail, Alethea? What kind of scam are you trying to run this time?"

"I forwarded my bills to you so you can pay that shit. I can't!"

"I'm not your husband anymore! I'm not responsible for you. At all!"

"You spent a lot of energy keeping me away from you, Carpious. I bet none of these folk know who you really are and where you *really* came from. Nah. They don't let folk like us move into lives like this. You just like me. What kinda con *you* running?"

"I'm nothing like you! I've *never* been an addict. And now you're coming around begging for money?"

"Not begging, motherfucka, *demanding*. You owe me. I helped *build* you. I was with you *before* you got that fuckin' fancy ass job. I stood by you. You either pay those medical bills and give me money for medicine or I tell yo' neighbors and yo' job all about Carpious Mightson. You pay or I say."

Carpious breathes heavily while staring at Alethea, deciding what he will do. His steel eyes and flaring nostrils do little to intimidate her as she purses her lips with her arms crossed staring back. Tense moments are measured by the steady and deep sound of Carpious breathing through his nostrils and then suddenly…

He angrily swings the front door open again.

"Get out before I call the police!"

Carpious is glaring at Alethea who has not moved when, from the corner of his eye, he sees Sydney and Solomon getting out of their car parked behind Alethea's.

Carpious' shift in behavior causes Alethea to move from her rebellious stance to see what has captured his immediate attention through the opened door. She mutters while nodding her head toward Sydney, "Oh, I see what's up."

Sydney approaches as Solomon runs ahead to greet Carpious exclaiming, "Carpious!!"

He grabs Carpious in a hug at the knees before Carpious can scoop him up.

Carpious interrupts his frown with a chuckled greeting, "Hey, Solo!"

Alethea glares toward Sydney approaching.

"I was 'bout to leave but this bitch got me hemmed in," she says softly to herself.

Sydney's casual dress of brown corduroy pants, orange cashmere sweater and jacket fail to disguise the fact that she is still quite an alluring and beautiful woman. She approaches Carpious and Alethea with no less confidence.

"Are we too early?" she innocently asks, looking to Alethea. She then addresses her presence with, "Hi."

Carpious reaches to put his hands on the small of Sydney's back with Solomon still attached to his legs.

"Sydney, this is Alethea, my ex-wife. She was just leaving."

Carpious looks at Alethea with no emotion.

Sydney nods her head in approval and politely smiles while reaching for Alethea's hand but Alethea responds coldly, "You got me blocked in."

Sydney responds, "O…kay. Sorry. Let me move my car. Excuse me for a moment, Carpious. It was nice meeting you, Alethea."

Alethea says nothing as Sydney walks back to her vehicle and backs out of the driveway to park on the street in front of the house.

She finally breaks her silence with, "This ain't ova! If that kid wasn't here, I would have much mo' to say, but I'm gonna be Christian-like on a Sunday and let ya'll have yo' nice dinner. You'll be hearing from me again."

Carpious stares at Alethea as she storms to her car and pulls out of the driveway. His jaws are tight enough to shatter his teeth while he stares coldly.

He says nothing.

~

Carpious waits at the door for Sydney to return to him and he hugs her before welcoming her in and closing the door. Solomon is still by his side.

"Ooooooh, it smells good in here!" Sydney sings enthusiastically as she walks in.

Solomon cocks his head and asks, "Carpious, can I go outside and play?"

Carpious answers, "Why don't we eat first and then y—"

Sydney interrupts softly but firmly, "Solomon, what did I tell you, young man? You can play after you eat."

"Yes, ma'am," Solomon drops his head both embarrassed and disappointed.

Carpious adds, "You can play in the living room until we call you for dinner. I have a new video game, and I want you to figure out how to play it so you can show me, and we can all play together later. Okay?"

Solomon comes back to life and excitedly asks his mother, "Mom, can I?"

Sydney chuckles and says, "Sure. What do you say?"

"Thank you, Carpious," Solomon shouts as he hugs Carpious' leg before bursting away into a run when his mother reminds him, "Walk!"

He stifles his run to a brisk walk trying to contain his excitement before turning the corner out of the view of his mother and continuing his race to the living room.

Sydney exhales and Carpious leads her into the kitchen, holding her hand.

Carpious, who is visibly disturbed, turns to Sydney with a furrowed brow and apologizes, "I'm sorry about that…on the porch. I had no idea she was coming or why. I haven't seen or heard from her in—"

Sydney interrupts Carpious by gripping his hand tight and putting her other hand over his mouth gently. She returns an unnaturally calm expression. "It's okay. We can talk about that later. She's gone now. Let's not let her ruin this any more than she already has."

Carpious protests, "Sydney, I think we need to talk about it now and get it over with, just in case she—"

Sydney continues to stare at Carpious with a patient calmness, as if she's trying to channel her calm energy into him. She quietly shakes her head back and forth. He locks gazes with her and pauses his protest.

He relaxes his resistance, "You're right. Another time."

~

Dinner was nearly perfect. Carpious, Sydney, and Solomon were like a real family minus the typical dysfunction that often appears during family gatherings. Conversation ranged from an eight-year-old's dissertation on the upcoming, exciting releases in the video game industry to two adults hypothesizing how the decline of the economy could be a good thing long-term if the government is forced to fix a system that has been broken for quite some time.

Carpious talked little of his job, but Sydney was a little more enthusiastic in talking about her own job as a nurse.

A discussion on the joys and woes of the health care industry concludes while Solomon has resigned from the dinner table and "boring adult conversation" to play outside with Haleigh and a few of the other neighborhood kids in Carpious' front yard.

Carpious sits at the head of the table and Sydney sits to his right. They are finishing a bottle of Riesling. Emptied plates lie before them and a candle that acted as the centerpiece has melted down almost halfway and continues to burn. Coltrane lightly plays in the background.

"We've been seeing each other for what, a year now? I think if you're lucky enough to marry me, you will be the designated cook in the family," Sydney teases.

"Whoa! Lucky enough?" Carpious laughs.

"Oh, did I say *lucky*? I meant *smart* enough."

They both laugh like old friends catching up, and Carpious places his hand on Sydney's. She leans in to kiss him.

Eleven months ago, they were a few hellos shy of being complete strangers. Carpious volunteered through a program at Admah City Community Church working with young boys of single mothers. The program was to assist boys from eight to twelve years of age to develop self-esteem and social skills by offering assistance in schoolwork, one-on-one outings, and relationship development. Carpious mentored two kids—Solomon and another one named Isaiah. Isaiah didn't stay in the program long because he and his mother moved away. It was Solomon's enthusiasm and relationship with Carpious that first drew Sydney's attention. Outings for two evolved into outings for three that then evolved into private outings for two with a babysitter to tend to the remainder.

Sydney was drawn to Carpious' gentle nature more than his strikingly handsome looks. The men she'd dated previously were usually in the health care field and she found them to be cocky, arrogant, too aggressive, or all of the above. And then there was her ex-husband. Carpious had assertiveness and strength, but he was also quiet and gentle at the same time. Because of this, she'd once again considered letting herself be vulnerable to be loved and loving again.

Eleven months later and evidently, her consideration had been received, processed, and unanimously accepted.

And they kiss.

CHAPTER FOUR

Light rain and diesel fumes accompany the moving truck parked backward in the driveway of 361 Mechi Lane. Curious neighbors peek from their warm, dry dwellings to learn more of the new occupant of the house that had been vacant for over a year.

The previous owners, a middle-aged married couple, fell on hard times when the husband was laid off from his job as a foreman at a mattress factory. The wife was physically disabled and unable to work more than a part-time job as a seamstress, and that yielded very little in the way of paying a mortgage and meeting other debts. The couple moved into a small apartment in a convenient location, sold their car, and put the house up for sale. The housing market was already slowing down due to a declining local economy and there had been very few serious inquiries since then.

Now, thirty-five-year-old Ian Kaplan was beneficiary to the misfortune that people weren't buying mattresses like they once did. He first registered an interest in the house over three months ago. With near-perfect credit, financing already secured, and a willingness to purchase the property at the asking price, the transaction should not have taken over three months, but Ian was no ordinary homebuyer. Serving eleven years in prison for having sex with a minor tends to make otherwise seamless transactions a little...complicated.

Admah City statutes mandate that Ian must register as a sex offender for fifteen years following his completed sentence and parole. His conviction carried with it a requirement to attend counseling on a regular and consistent basis during those fifteen years. As a registered sex offender, he is unable to come within 750 yards of where children or minors may congregate—a school, playground, daycare, the back of an ice cream truck. That was the main obstacle to his home purchase. He had to make certain that there were no laws prohibiting him from moving to Mechi Lane. Though there are children that live there, there would have to be a playground or similar area to consider them *congregating* in one area. That legal loophole and a judge signing off on it gave Ian permission to purchase the property.

Finally the day has come. Cool December rain falls more consistently as Ian carries small, neatly packed and labeled boxes from the cabin of the truck to the welcoming doors of his new home. His original plan of moving under the cover of night was interrupted by heavy rain and a mild consideration for not disturbing his new neighbors. As soon as the rain slacked off, he decided that it was best to get as much out of the truck as possible. The process would probably be over in an hour or so with two more men to assist, but Ian doesn't seem to have many friends—at least none who are willing to help him move furniture in the rain in the early hours of the morning.

Additionally, those who have known Ian for a long time would probably say that he was always a bit of a recluse. In high school, he was that geeky kid who ate in the cafeteria alone or with the other maladjusted misfits. Whereas pubescent years for a boy are typically hormone-induced pursuits of girls and instant gratification, Ian was socially inept around the opposite sex. His public and humiliating attempts at expressing his attraction to any particular girl only served to make him more awkward as time passed. But then somewhere between high school and age twenty-three, he got the guts to talk to a girl. Unfortunately, she was only thirteen.

~

Twelve years ago, Ian was beginning an eleven-year sentence for being, as his lawyer pleaded, a "late bloomer with bad judgment." The court had another name for him: sick.

Ian was sentenced to serve eleven years at Siddim Valley State Prison, a medium-security prison that is thirty-five miles south of Admah City. Medium-security prisons are where a majority of the United States prison population is incarcerated. Siddim Valley State is not unlike most medium-security prisons—underfunded, understaffed, and dangerously overcrowded. With the capacity to house 1,100 inmates and employ 340 security officers, the tax payers' dollars give prisoners access to literacy programs, basic education and GED preparation, college and vocational courses, alcohol and substance counseling, anger management therapy, religious communities, and physical recreation. To those law-abiding or lucky individuals who will never be isolated during a lockdown following the murder of a fellow inmate or some other altercation, the prison curriculum may appear to be a moderately nice resort. Siddim Valley State is far from a resort or a "bad boy" retreat. It's a hornet's nest of con artists and abusers where fairness is an ideal that is best forgotten. It's a lion's den where even peaceful sleep is elusive and rare. It's a tangled and forgotten forest where predators learn to become more efficient predators and the lines are blurred as to whether the most dangerous predators are the inmates or the correctional officers. Ian may have been considered a predator on the outside, but inside prison he was immediately labeled the prey.

His small size, criminal inexperience, and timid nature made him an immediate target during his first thirty days in the "fishbowl." The "fishbowl" is the nickname of the temporary holding cell where new prisoners are placed during processing before they are assigned permanent living quarters. Psychological evaluations, medical screenings, and thorough emasculation by the correctional officers and faculty is all seemingly necessary "processing" before the new prisoners are released into the general prison population. The "fishbowl" is also in plain view of everyone, so the predators may select their prey in advance.

Ian was eventually released into the general prison population and tethered with a cellmate who called Skidmark—or Skid for short. His real name was Malcolm Martin but no one uses his real name in prison. Evidently, the nickname was given or self-imposed due to his extremely dark skin and thin frame. Despite Skid's stature, Ian was still afraid of him and Skid used

Ian's fear to his advantage as he schooled Ian on prison life. Because Ian was white, he would automatically be in danger of being declared "territory" by the blacks or the Mexicans. Territory declaration was most often acted out in the form of a brutal gang rape. Skid told Ian that he could offer him protection from those atrocities for $150 a month. While he didn't look like he could do much in the way of protection, Skid went on to explain to Ian how he was connected to the blacks and how money was more powerful and convincing than size.

Ian was book smart and had come from a wealthy family, but he'd never had the opportunity or interest to wander onto paths in life that would have required him to possess street smarts. He agreed to protection under the terms that Skid presented and, though no one ever came to visit him, he had access to his accounts. And so his fear devolved to nervousness, which devolved to complacency in a matter of three months. Complacency is not a quality advantageous to surviving in prison.

The three hours that Ian was not locked in his cell were often spent with Skid and the blacks in his proximity. Whether it was in the cafeteria or on the yard or in the rec room watching TV, Ian felt irrationally "safe." He didn't talk to anyone or make eye contact with anyone other than Skid. One random day, Skid changed the terms of their protection agreement without Ian's knowledge.

Word had gotten out, probably from some talkative and bored correctional officer, that Ian was serving time for statutory rape of a minor—a thirteen-year-old helpless girl. Though Siddim Valley State is an institution of violent offenders on whom justice has been exacted, there seems to be some line of morality that you don't cross, even as a hardened criminal. You don't kill your mother and you *don't* touch kids.

Ironic is what it is. Ian was complacent and ignorant and innocent as he sat watching Jerry Springer reruns in the rec room one afternoon. Suddenly and quietly, those who were sitting around him got up and left. Ian's attention was drawn to this mass exodus when he noticed Skid was also leaving without a word or a glance. Ian got up to leave with him, but a group of about a dozen large dark men blocked his exit. Ian called to Skid who never turned to acknowledge him. Then Ian desperately looked around for the correctional officer who was also suddenly absent. Then he knew.

The first blow landed across his face and nearly took his head off. Ian fell to the ground and was conscious but dazed; the second blow loosened at least five teeth from the front of his mouth. He gagged and almost choked on his own teeth and blood but was gripped from behind. A fist was shoved into his ribs similar to the Heimlich maneuver performed on choking victims, forcing him to spit all contents from his mouth. And then stark and sudden panic caused him to vomit contents from his stomach, as he was held in place over the back of a chair and savagely raped. He couldn't cry for help, because the men who were not violating him from behind or holding him down were forcing their engorged penises into his mouth. They were barking at him to suck and if he didn't, they would kick and punch him in his torso until he complied. This went on for what felt like hours until Ian lost consciousness and his anus gushed blood. No correctional officer came to interrupt or rescue, and there was no Skid to offer protection.

~

But that was then. Twelve years ago. Now, his rain-soaked hair and cramping fingers indicate freedom as he moves back and forth in silence emptying the contents of the moving truck into his new home. Falling rain accompanied by mist drenches his clothes as a hint of the early morning winter air sends chills through him that cause him to grit his teeth, which are now a collection of expensive porcelain veneers and dental implants.

Ian begins to breathe heavier as he travels back and forth and realizes that he may need to slow down a bit. Asthma is a condition that surfaced in prison somewhere in between infirmary visits. He stops just short of clearing the truck and leans on the box of books that he was practically dragging. Looking past his yard at the other houses around him, he sees little activity beyond his own. One of his neighbors is standing on her front lawn with her hands on her hips, overlooking a small dog that is sniffing around the lawn to decide where it will lay its early morning treasure. Ian chuckles to himself as he suspects his neighbor's duties are more a ruse to spy on him than to allow her dog to relieve itself. He stares in her direction while still leaning on the box as if he's waiting to catch a glimpse of eye contact with his neighbor. It never happens. She calls to her dog some indistinguishable name and they go back inside without her acknowledging Ian's presence.

Ian exhales deeply and stands to hoist the box of books once again. He grips below the weight and musters enough energy to toss the hefty weight into his arms. As he does so, the rain-moistened box loses its integrity under the burden of books and spills its contents from beneath. A mass of books fans out and falls at Ian's feet as he holds the emptied cardboard container.

"Shit," he breathes.

He kneels to quickly collect the books into his arms to save them from further water damage. As he stacks all that he can hurry into the house, one book catches his attention and gives him momentary pause—a weathered and dog-eared edition of a leather Bible with half the cover missing. At that, his frustrated expression is transformed into a gentle and thoughtful calm. This ragged book was his solace in prison. Past the rape, the beatings, the humiliations and double-crosses, these pages indicated that forgiveness for what he'd done was possible.

Ian would not describe himself as religious or pious, but when a man is torn down to nothing, he needs something to resurrect him if he chooses to live. He needs a kind of hope. He needs the peace of a second chance.

~

The skies yawn awake from a cold and damp slumber as dozens of pairs of headlights begin to litter the highway for rush hour traffic. The ground is wet with the evidence of something more significant than dew, while the rain has subsided for the moment. Peace and quiet is agitated by accelerating engines, car horns, and the thud of someone's music escaping from behind the closed doors and glass.

Off the highway on an access road tucked away out of view sits a twenty-four-hour diner named Benny's Roadside Diner. Carpious has been meeting Russell Moser there periodically for breakfast for the past eight years. What started as a means for them to study the Bible together has since evolved into a friendship.

Seated in the back of the diner past empty tables and chairs, the duo is waiting for their food orders to arrive.

"How's work been treating you?" Russell predictably initiates.

Carpious empties three packets of sugar into a cup of coffee, answering, "I can't complain at all. Or I should say that I *won't* complain at all? I am blessed beyond measure with this job. I mean, the traveling sometimes takes its toll, but I'm in a place that I would have never thought possible ten years ago. How's *your* week been?"

Russell laughs, "Well, I *will* complain. This week, my job has *sucked*."

Carpious looks up from stirring cream into his coffee and studies Russell's face, unsure of whether he should laugh as well. Russell chuckles some more and Carpious joins in with an uncomfortable smile.

Russell takes a long sip of orange juice before continuing.

"I love people and I love serving God by ministering to people's needs, but sometimes…sometimes I need a break from all of the ugliness and depravity that I have to hear about and see. Sometimes *I* need a counseling session. That's why I value these times when we can get together and I don't have to be Pastor Russell. I can just be…Russell."

"Well, you're not the only one to benefit from these meetings. Talking to you always makes me feel…" Carpious looks down at the empty table in front of him while pondering what word to say next, "…accepted," he finishes as he looks up again and stares back at Russell with intensity.

"You *are* accepted, brother. How many times have you heard me say that we *all* have our issues? Everyone wants to belong to something. Everyone has at least one insecurity or secret that they struggle with or try to keep hidden from view for fear that if anyone finds out, they'll be exiled from the caste of humanity. No one is perfect and put together right. If we were, I would be out of a job."

Carpious smiles and sips coffee as their waitress returns to the table with plates of food.

"Alright, gentlemen, I have a Western omelet with a side of fruit."

Carpious raises his finger and the waitress places the plate in front of him.

"And I have scrambled eggs, turkey bacon, and waffles."

She places two plates in front of Russell.

"Will there be anything else, gentlemen?" she says with her hands on her hips.

"No, thank you. This looks great," Russell answers while unrolling silverware from a napkin.

Carpious shakes his head and says, "Thank you."

The waitress leaves and Carpious continues, "It doesn't matter that *everyone* has insecurities. Some things are acceptable blemishes while others are not. Some issues are not regarded as bad while others are fixated and focused on. People have a tendency to be so judgmental against some issues. You would think men and women of God would have a different perspective, but a lot of them are worse than those who don't even *know* God. To them, some sins are worse than others. For example, no one ever looks at fat people with the same disgust that they would look at...say...a promiscuous person. They would swoop down on that promiscuous person with extreme judgment and name-calling and ostracism, while the fat person would be forgiven and accepted as one of them. Fornication and gluttony are *both* wrong according to the Bible."

"People, whether they know God or not, don't want to be reminded of their wrongdoings. When they see that promiscuous person, they see their own failures. They see their own sin. The fat person may not offend some, but others may have a different perspective. You can't stop people from thinking what they're going to think, Carpious. You can only control you."

Carpious smiles uneasily in resolve. "I guess."

Russell looks at Carpious with a concentrated glare, unconvinced that he is really receiving his words with encouragement, so he changes the course of the conversation with, "Shall we bless the food?"

"Yes! The smell of this has my mouth watering and ready to go. I'll pray."

Both men bow their heads as Carpious recites words of thanks.

CHAPTER FIVE

Secrets. Everyone has them. The light of day and truth reveal some secrets to be nagging obsessions or habits, while other secrets may be as incriminating as a literal decaying skeleton in one's closet.

Surprises. They're like secrets but are usually tied to some positive outcome. Whether they come hidden in colorful wrapping paper or some intended misdirection, most people like surprises. Carpious sits in his car in the parking lot of Mercy General Hospital as he waits for Sydney's shift to end. He has a surprise for her.

As he sits reclined in the driver's seat, Carpious browses through songs on a CD trying to find the right tune to listen to as he waits. He's only been parked for ten minutes but is already growing restless. The slow and dismal air of Nina Simone singing "Everything Must Change" holds his attention for a moment until he hears the background chatter of people laughing and talking. He suddenly sits up to see a group of women walking toward his vehicle, but Sydney isn't with them. He looks at his watch and relaxes back into his previous posture.

Nina Simone continues to wail, "There are not many things in life one can be sure of except rain comes from the clouds, sun lights up the sky, hummingbirds fly, winter turns to spring, a wounded heart will heal…oh, but never much too soon. No one and nothing goes unchanged. The young become the old and mysteries do unfold for that's the way of time. No one and nothing stays unchanged."

Carpious listens to the words and music with his eyes closed and remains still and expressionless as if asleep. Then, just as suddenly as before, he springs up and turns to see Sydney and two other women leaving the building.

He stirs into action as he removes the key from the ignition and reaches to the passenger side to retrieve a bouquet of carnations of varying colors wrapped in red-tinted cellophane. He steps from his car and quietly closes the door while smoothing any wrinkles from his clothing. A smile appears across his face as he strides toward Sydney who has not noticed him yet. His towering appearance is accentuated by black slacks and a pressed white shirt with threaded patterns only visible when the light reflects upon it a certain way. He's also wearing black leather boots and a beige tweed blazer that has cinnamon and brown woven into it. He smells faintly of patchouli and lemongrass while his cleanly shaven face has the subtle glow that only shea butter can lend.

He is about twenty feet away before Sydney looks up and sees Carpious walking toward her with flowers and a smile. She stops in mid-step and mid-sentence and stares silently with her hand covering her mouth in surprise. The women who are with her look at her before they also notice Carpious who has slowed his approach.

He nods and acknowledges the other two women,

"Ladies. Hello. Might I be graced with the company of your coworker?"

"Certainly," one woman giggles.

"We'll talk to you tomorrow, girl," the other one hums. The women walk away giggling and talking.

Carpious reaches out to hug Sydney who still appears to be in a jovial state of shock. He hugs her tightly and she returns the affection.

"I wanted to surprise you. Are you surprised?" he whispers.

He releases her and puts the bouquet of flowers in front of her. "These are for you. I recall that you love carnations," he says.

"Oh, Carpious...I...I don't know what to say. This is so sweet. No one has ever shown up with flowers. You are my knight in shining tweed," she purrs as she strokes his chest.

She looks down and buries her face in the bouquet. "These are so beautiful."

"They pale in comparison to you, dear Sydney. And they're just the beginning."

Carpious opens the passenger side of his car to allow her in. She kisses him before taking a seat.

Once Carpious is back in the car and restarts the engine, he finishes sharing with Sydney. "I arranged a babysitter tonight for Solomon. I'm going to take you home so you can wash off the day and then I'm taking you out for a night of music and dinner."

"Carpious! You are so amazing. What's the occasion?"

"*You* are the occasion. I just realized the other day how important you are to me, and I never want you to have to wonder or guess how I feel."

Sydney beams to herself and smells the flowers again.

"Also, I know that you've been catching the train because your car was giving you trouble. I'm going to let you use my car next week, and I'll take yours in to get it looked at. It's too cold for you to have to walk to the train station."

Sydney looks away from Carpious still smiling. A lone tear streams down her face and many others follow after it.

"Thank you, Carpious. You just don't know how much this means to me. Thank you so much."

~

The garage door squeal welcomes Drew Janson home as his car pulls into the driveway. Once the car is fully inside and almost as soon as it completely opens, the garage door reverses its ascension to close. The garage is crowded with disassembled furniture, used toys, and stackable plastic storage boxes. The walls are lined with shelves of more boxes and an assortment of garden and power tools. Overhead is a dim and flickering row of fluorescent lights. As Drew steps out of the car, the smell of dinner greets him. He looks at his watch as he closes the car door and his complacent look reveals nothing of whether he's happy to be home or if he's bracing for some confrontation.

He turns the doorknob and opens the door into the kitchen without the assistance of a key. A burst of humid heat confronts him as he walks inside. The kitchen is void of any activity, and the only sign of life is the hum of the dishwasher. On the stove is a plate loosely wrapped in foil that reminds him he is severely late for dinner.

"Lela? Haleigh?" he timidly calls out.

No one answers as he continues through the kitchen toward the hallway. The faint sound of his daughter, Haleigh, splashing and giggling in the bathtub greets him as he nears the bathroom. He peers through the doorway.

"Hello, ladies," he greets.

"Daddy!" Haleigh screams in excitement.

"Hey, pumpkin. Were you a good girl today?" he asks, not yet addressing his wife, Lela, who is sitting on the edge of the tub with a sudsy washcloth.

"Yes," Haleigh's excitement turns sheepish as she looks at her mom.

Lela looks at Haleigh and directs, "Tell Daddy what happened at dinner."

"I didn't want to eat my broccoli," Haleigh shyly says with pouted lips.

Lela turns her attention to Drew who is leaning against the door frame with his arms crossed. "Haleigh refused to eat broccoli because she wanted to wait until Daddy got home to eat with her. But Daddy didn't call to say that he would be late from work. Daddy didn't call at all. So Haleigh wouldn't finish her dinner," Lela calmly states, glaring at Drew.

Drew looks at Haleigh and his face turns apologetic, "Honey, Daddy's sorry that he's late for dinner. I'll make it up to you, okay?"

Haleigh nods and returns to smiling and splashing in the water. Lela looks at Drew who fails to acknowledge her as he leaves to go to the bedroom. She turns her attention back to Haleigh. "Come on, baby. Let's get you out of the tub and into the bed."

Drew flips the light on in the bedroom, unbuttoning his shirt as he walks across the room into the master bathroom. He stands in front of the mirror that dominates most of the wall opposite of the door and sniffs the shirt right before he takes it off. The scent startles him and he immediately rips the shirt off and stuffs it in the clothes hamper underneath clothes that are already there.

"Where've you been all this time, Drew?" a voice asks him from behind. He jumps back from the hamper startled but composes himself just as quickly. Lela is standing directly behind him in the bathroom doorway.

"What are you doing sneaking up on people?" he defensively snaps.

"For some reason, I don't think I'm the one doing the sneaking around here," Lela says.

"What are you talking about?" Drew asks as he brushes past Lela to go back into the bedroom. He sits down on the neatly made bed and diverts his attention to the removal of his shoes and socks.

"You know what I'm talking about, Drew. What happened to calling your family to say that you're going to be late for dinner? Or that you're not coming at all?"

Silence.

Lela continues louder, "I don't know where you've been going after work, but you've been getting later and later for the past couple of weeks. And today you don't even call?"

Drew raises his hands in defeat, "I'm sorry. Things have been getting crazy at work and I was inconsiderate not to call. Time caught up with me. I'm sorry, okay?"

"No! You don't *get* to be the victim here," Lela angrily points her finger in Drew's face. "While you're off God knows where, your daughter is crying and wondering where her daddy is. And her mommy can't tell her because Mommy doesn't know!"

Silence. Drew is looking down at the floor, defeated.

"I don't know what you're going through, but you better get over it quickly. You said you wanted this baby too. It's time for you to stop thinking about yourself and consider your family, Drew Janson."

Drew rebounds, "All I *do* is think about this family! I work hard *because* of this family. You think I like working late every day? You think I don't want to stay home and enjoy spending time with my daughter sometimes? Well, I do. And all you do is complain about what I do and what I don't. And what I do is never good enough. I'm tired of this, Lela. I want to feel appreciated and not come home to *this* every night."

Drew begins putting his shoes and socks back on. He gets up and yanks a T-shirt from a drawer while Lela stands with her hands on her hips. He storms out of the room.

Lela calls out, "Drew…"

Drew storms past Haleigh's room. Haleigh sees the blur of her father and calls out, "Daddy?"

The only response Haleigh or Lela gets is a slammed door and the squeal of the garage door opening.

~

Translated to English from Akan, a language spoken in Ghana, *sankofa* means to go back and take or reclaim. The symbol or icon often associated with it is of a bird reaching backward holding an egg. That theme and aesthetic subtlety can be seen throughout the restaurant that Carpious has taken Sydney to and it is of the same name. Sankofa's owners are of Kenyan heritage, and Carpious befriended them at a networking function last year. The unassuming, eclectic restaurant has been a part of downtown Admah City for a little over two years in the artsy warehouse and gallery district. Live music is played Wednesday through Sunday and is usually of a jazz or acoustic variety. The ambience is modern with low lighting and minimalist décor throughout.

The house lights brighten as the lead player for the band announces a thirty-minute break before they will continue their next set. Sydney looks across the white cloth-covered table at Carpious and smiles.

Carpious smiles back just before stuffing the last of the basil potatoes into his mouth.

"Carpious, this place is awesome. How did you find out about it?" Sydney asks.

Carpious manages through chewing, "Umm…I met the owners last year. They were hyping it up to my company, and I've read a lot of great reviews about it since then."

"My steak was delicious. I see yours must have been good too."

Carpious finishes chewing. "Yes…mmmmmm…the tenderloins melted in my mouth." Carpious grabs his napkin from his lap and wipes the corners of his mouth as he clears his throat. "I've gotta confess though…I had ulterior motives for this evening."

"Oh?" Sydney responds.

"Yeah. I know that the last few weeks have seen me distant from you. I've been traveling what feels like non-stop, to the point that I wasn't sure if I was coming or going. We haven't really had the chance to spend quality time with each other like in the beginning. I may be getting a bit of a break from the traveling for a couple of months and I wanted you to know that I want to take advantage of that by spending as much quality time with you as possible. I think you are an amazing woman and I don't want to lose you because I fail to show you that."

"Awww, that's so thoughtful of you. I guess you were listening to what I was hinting at, huh?"

Carpious laughs, "A little bit."

Sydney continues, "Well, you know Solomon adores you almost as much as I do. He would love to see more of you too. Christmas is coming up. Why don't we share it?"

"Absolutely. As a matter of fact, why don't you let me keep him tomorrow night? It will give you some time to yourself and he and I can indulge ourselves with Godzilla movies, lots of junk food, and staying up late," Carpious suggests.

"You're *such* a keeper. I need a break, and he'll love it! Deal!"

Carpious lifts his glass and drinks water from the melted ice cubes. Sydney reaches across the table and grasps Carpious' hand. "When you and Alethea were married, did you ever talk about having kids?"

Carpious puts the glass down and looks away with an intense and thoughtful expression. He is silent for a long moment before hesitantly looking back at Sydney who is still holding his hand and looking at him warmly. "The short time that I was married was spent realizing that I made a mistake marrying someone out of obligation. Alethea was not who she professed to be in the beginning and when I found out who she really was, she almost dragged me down with her. Her drug addiction and dangerous temper…I was trying to get my life together with a new job and all, but she didn't care about anything. No, we never even considered the idea of having a kid."

He looks more intently at Sydney and grasps her hand with his other one. "But I love kids. I want to be to *them* what no one was to or for *me*," Carpious confesses with passion.

"What was your father like? Was he around?" Sydney asks.

Carpious looks away in an attempt to hide his obvious shift in emotion at the question. He rubs his broad face as if there is stubble there and ponders for a moment.

He whispers, "What was he like? He wasn't. My father was around long enough to tear my life apart. That's why I want to help all the kids I can. I want them to know that every man doesn't come along, screw their lives up, and then run away."

"Do *you* know that, Carpious? Now? Do you know that every man or woman doesn't leave you?" Sydney asks as she leans in to Carpious. "No matter what you've been through, I won't leave you. No matter what you've done, I won't judge you. I'm not going anywhere."

Carpious looks at Sydney and smiles, wanting to believe every word. But he doesn't.

CHAPTER SIX

Carpious had seen many Christmas Eves—forty-five in fact—but most of his adult life was absent of the naïveté and excitement that can come from a child whose unlimited imagination swells with Christmas Day anticipation. Carpious and Sydney had previously discussed sharing Christmas festivities at Carpious' house to Solomon's glee. Several brightly wrapped gifts of varying sizes and shapes are piled under a freshly cut Fraser fir trimmed with lights fading from dim to bright rather than blinking erratically. The smell of sap mingles with the scent of cinnamon, inducing a spirit of calm and relaxation for Carpious and Sydney while quickening the pulse of Solomon who is in bed but finding it difficult to slip into any form of unconsciousness or still thought.

Carpious and Sydney sit in a darkened living room in one corner of the couch, snuggled beside one another watching the end of *It's a Wonderful Life*. The sound on the television is low enough so as to not disturb Solomon down the hallway but loud enough that its audience of two can make out the dialogue. Sydney is such a fan of the movie that she could probably follow along and quote the movie even if the sound were set to mute. It was her suggestion to spend the evening watching traditional Christmas movies like *Miracle on 34th Street*, *A Christmas Story*, and *It's a Wonderful Life* while sipping on seasonal elixirs and munching on various holiday confections. Carpious had been content in the past to listen to music in the background while nodding off on the couch to football recaps on the sports channels.

"Mommy," a voice sings in a whisper from behind them.

Sydney abruptly turns, while Carpious is a little slower to respond as evidence that he was continuing some part of his tradition of nodding to sleep on the couch.

"I can't sleep," Solomon whines as he rubs his eyes looking in the direction of the Christmas tree littered with gifts beneath. He's wearing light blue one-piece footed pajamas with Spider-Man patterns on them.

"Honey, the sooner you sleep, the sooner Santa can come. He won't come if you're awake," Sydney reasons.

"But I see presents already…"

Carpious smiles to himself as he gets up. "I got him," he whispers to Sydney as he runs his hand along her shoulder. "Come on, Buddy. Those are *pre*-Santa presents. Santa Claus is bringing the *big* presents, but only after you go to sleep," Carpious says to Solomon as he lifts him in the air and turns him upside down. Happy shrills of an already excited seven-year-old fade down the hallway into one of Carpious' guestrooms.

Sydney smiles and nestles back into the couch once more with the confidence that if anyone can bargain Solomon to sleep, Carpious can and will.

The movie ends before Carpious returns. Sydney sits up to allow for him to resume his previous position.

"Down for the count," Carpious reports.

"What did you do?" Sydney asks.

"I gave him a sip of eggnog with rum," Carpious jokes.

"No, really."

"I told him that I would wake him up as soon as Santa left."

"And that did it?" Sydney asks surprised.

Carpious looks at her and hesitates before laughing and then subsiding to seriousness. "I told him I would be here when he wakes up."

"Cool," Sydney says as she nestles back into the arms of Carpious, smiling at the sensitivity and depth of his statement.

~

Haleigh had already drifted to sleep following her warm bath and Christmas bedtime story. Her mother had assured her that Santa would come and that her daddy would be there when she woke up.

Lela had developed the habit of busying herself with household chores to distract her mind from wondering where her husband was during his unexplained absences. She knew that he wasn't working late. She'd grown numb to the response of worrying for his safety since she figured she'd hear of his fate quicker if there was an emergency than she would by getting a voluntary call from him. She pays little regard to the television supplying background noise as she empties the clothes hamper onto the floor of their bedroom to sort clothes to wash.

For Lela, pregnancy has brought with it an irrational appetite, a higher than normal emotional sensitivity, and an acute while annoying sense of smell. To avoid nausea that would likely follow the smell of mildewed towels and musty shirts, she stands with her hands on her hips and sorts through the dirty clothes with her feet.

"What's that smell?" she mumbles to herself surprised.

She stoops to pick up one of Drew's dress shirts. The assault of a woman's perfume that is not her own emanates from the shirt. She frantically looks the shirt over seeing no further evidence of the woman, but it is already too late.

Lela drops back onto the bed and begins to cry.

~

Stillness. The home and guests of Carpious Mightson are asleep. Solomon is nestled in the covers that Carpious had previously tucked him under. Carpious and Sydney have fallen asleep on the couch beneath a throw in front of the television that is no more than a dim dancing light to them now. Quiet. Not so much as a reticent snore looms in the warm air. The television is set to mute. Perhaps at the conclusion of a sleepy bathroom trip, Sydney silenced it so as to not disturb Carpious and then went back to sleep with him where she lay on his chest.

Then as sudden and unexpected as a fire alarm, the phone rings blaringly. Sydney jumps up.

"Carpious. Carpious, the phone," she nudges him awake as the phone continues to ring.

Carpious stumbles across the room and picks up the phone.

"H-hello?" he sleepily greets as he squints at his watch. It's 11:35pm. "Lela?" he asks after listening for a few moments.

"Lela…Lela, calm down. Where is Drew? O-okay. It's okay. I'll be right over…Okay. I'll be right there."

Carpious hangs up the phone with a concerned frown. He looks to Sydney who has a worried look on her face. "My neighbor next door is going into labor and wants me to take her to the emergency room. Her husband's not home, and she can't get him on the phone. Do you mind staying here until I call you?"

"Sweetie, I'm a nurse. Is there anything I can do? I can drive her to the hospital."

"No, I have it. I wouldn't want you both out alone at this hour and I don't think it's a good idea for us all to go because we'd have to wake Solomon. Would you just stay here with him, please?"

"Of course, sweetie. Let me get your jacket."

Carpious begins putting on his shoes as Sydney hastens out of the room. She returns with his jacket and hat.

"Call me as soon as you get there," she says as she hugs and kisses him and then closes the door behind him.

~

A drowsy garage door opens as Carpious anxiously waits to back his car out into the driveway. He accelerates backward into the quiet street and whips his car into the Loomis' driveway so that he's now facing the street. Right as Carpious opens the door to step out, a set of bright lights appear in front of him, temporarily blinding him. He slowly steps out of the car, squinting with one hand holding the car door and the other hand raised in front of his face to block the bright light. He stands there for a tense moment with the engine and heat still running.

The headlights dim at the same time a voice calls out, "Carpious? What are you doing here?"

Carpious begins to walk toward the source of the voice that is revealed to be Drew as he regains his full capacity of sight.

"Drew? Where have you been? Your wife said she's been trying to reach you all night," Carpious announces.

Drew and Carpious are face-to-face now and Drew's previous look of surprise turns to territorial defensiveness.

"Where have I *been*? Carpious, I don't see where that is any of *your* business."

Surprised at the rude retort, Carpious snaps back, "It's *my* business when *your* pregnant wife calls me late at night to take her to the emergency room because she can't find *you*!"

Drew withdraws his defensive stance. "Wait, what? Is Lela sick? What happened?"

"I'm not sure. She called in a panic because she thought she was going into labor and she said she wanted me to take her to the emergency room. That's what I was about to do when you finally showed up."

Drew runs toward the house in a panic, but Carpious grabs Drew by the arm and looks at him intensely, saying nothing, as if he's searching for some confession or truth. Drew returns the stare frowning and without blinking and jerks his arm from Carpious.

"What are you doing? Get your hands off me!" Drew snaps.

Carpious watches Drew storm toward the house as Lela opens the door.

"Lela, are you okay?" Drew asks.

"Drew! I'm scared. Where've you been? I'm bleeding and cramping and you weren't here!" Lela begins crying.

"It's okay, honey. Where's Haleigh?"

"She's sleeping. I didn't want to scare her."

"Come on. Let me get you to the car and then I'll get Haleigh. Everything is going to be okay. I'm here."

Drew puts his arms around Lela to steady her weight as her crying fades to a whimper and slowly guides her out the door, down three steps, and past Carpious who is standing by his car watching as if waiting to assist in some way.

Drew places her in the car and heads back inside for Haleigh. As soon as he's inside, Carpious hurries to the passenger side where Lela is seated. He taps on the window and she rolls it down.

"Haleigh can stay with me until you guys get everything under control. It's Christmas Eve. There's no reason to upset her. Everything is going to be okay. I'm sure of it," he reassures Lela with his hand on her shoulder.

"That's a good idea, Carpious. Thank you."

Carpious looks up to see Drew carrying a still-sleeping Haleigh loosely wrapped in a blanket. He walks up to Drew and reaches for Haleigh.

"Let me help you, Drew. Haleigh can stay with me. Lela needs your full attention right now."

Drew, with jaws clenched, says nothing as he looks past Carpious toward the car where Lela is waiting and reluctantly offers Haleigh to him.

"Let me grab Haleigh's clothes and some of her gifts."

As Drew rushes back into the house, Carpious places the limp seven-year-old in the backseat of his car and buckles her in. Drew reappears with an armful of boxed gifts and a tote bag and places them in the trunk of Carpious' car.

"Thank you, Carpious," Drew mumbles as he hastens to his own car.

The bright lights flash as the car backs out of the driveway and drives off.

Carpious stands on the driver's side of his car with the engine and heater still running. He whispers without emotion into the darkness of night, "You're welcome."

~

Seven and a half hours later, Carpious is still awake, sitting on the couch with the television droning in the background. His thoughts are nowhere but his body won't let him sleep. He hears Solomon and Haleigh stirring down the hallway and the voice of Sydney directing their Christmas morning excitement, "Brush your teeth first and *then* we will open presents."

Sydney had taken Haleigh to bed with her in the second guestroom and was diligent to not have Haleigh awaken first wondering where her parents were. So the past few hours, Sydney slept lightly, keeping Haleigh close to her so that she would wake if Haleigh stirred.

When Haleigh's eyes open to Sydney, she isn't startled or confused. She simply asks, "Where's my mommy?"

"Mommy and Daddy had to go to the doctor because Mommy wasn't feeling well, but they'll be home soon. And *you* get to have Christmas with Carpious until they get back."

"Yay!" Haleigh exclaims, waking Solomon in the other room who appears at the doorway just as excited.

"Is it Christmas yet?" he asks.

"Brush your teeth first and *then* we will open presents."

The phone rings once and Carpious picks it up before it can ring a second time.

"Hello?"

"Carpious?" It's Drew on the other end. "Lela is going to be fine. The doctor said that stress instigated early labor, but she's not in danger of miscarriage as long as she follows his order of bed rest until the baby arrives in March. Thank you for helping out. We'll be home by noon."

Sydney walks into the living room and sees Carpious holding the phone to his ear listening. She appears anxious to know that Lela is okay. Carpious responds to Drew while at the same time answering Sydney, "Good to hear that Lela is going to be okay, Drew. We'll see you two in a few hours. Merry Christmas."

CHAPTER SEVEN

Alethea Mightson takes a long last drag on a cigarette that is not much more than a filter as she sits on cobblestone steps bundled in a puffy pink coat with its furry-edged hood pulled over her head. She's huddled in a crouched position with her head ducked low in an attempt to ward off the January wind that rushes past her. At her feet are at least a dozen cigarette butts, indicating that she's been sitting on this stoop braving the bitter cold for at least an hour. She grinds the cigarette butt into the ground alongside its departed siblings and looks around. It's quiet, cold, and overcast, but she seems to have an intent purpose and is willing to wait.

Across the street from where Alethea is sitting are three small kids chasing each other with sticks. They are bundled in winter coats and hats, but the winter temperature and their restrictive dress seem to have little bearing on their merriment as they giggle, scream, and chase each other at random and without logic. Althea looks in their direction occasionally, but her mind is elsewhere as she stares blankly. Aside from the giggles and screams of children, there is little background noise to accompany this winter afternoon.

The sound of an approaching car breaks Alethea's meditation, and she looks up to see a silver Honda Accord slowly pulling into the driveway in front of her. The vehicle stops short of entering the garage door that has begun to open and parks prematurely. Carpious gets out and slams the car door. The cold wind greets him. He looks around cautiously before walking around the car to approach Alethea. He sees the children playing and then looks toward Bernie's house, but there is no sign of Bernie. For that matter, there is no sign of any other neighbors that may have witnessed the intrusion sitting on his front steps. Carpious straightens his posture walks toward Alethea with no expression on his face and says nothing. He stops in front of her, looming with an intensity and silence that would be threatening to anyone who doesn't know him. Alethea returns his stare with an arrogant smirk before breaking the silence.

"How you doin', Carpious?"

Carpious sighs, "Alethea, why are you here? What is it that you want?"

"I already told you what I want. And I *told* you I would be back. You done had plenty of time to think about my request. Shit! You done had more than enough time to go on 'head and pay them bills that came to you. I see you ain't though. I got refused some of my prescriptions until that balance is paid. I need my medicine."

Carpious smirks as he shifts his weight onto the foot planted on the step in front of Alethea, who is still seated. His hands are stuffed in his pockets, as all that's protecting him from the arctic wind is a tweed blazer that complements khaki slacks and a starched, white shirt.

"That's not my problem, Alethea. You're a grown woman who should be responsible for herself. You're *not* my wife and you're *not* my child. There are plenty of clinics around town that will help you get your medicine free of charge. I'm not going to help you, so you might as well walk back to whatever den of thieves you scammed your way out of."

Alethea abruptly stands, clearly agitated. Her volume and gestures betray her previous coolness. "Oh, see? See how cold-hearted you is, motherfucka. I come tryin' to be quiet and not disturb yo' peaceful neighborhood and you go startin' shit with the insults. I didn't come to fight. I came for what's rightfully mine and you wanna act like you betta than me."

Carpious maintains his smirk with a confidence that he's in control of the scenario. In a calm tone he says, "Okay, Alethea. Let's talk this out for once and for all."

He pulls his hand out of his pocket and points a set of keys in the direction of the garage door. As the garage door whines to a close, Carpious walks up the steps past Alethea to unlock the front door. He gestures for her to come inside.

~

"Have a seat," Carpious says as he moves through the darkened house turning on lights. Alethea removes her coat and sits on one end of the large couch in the living room.

"Can I get you anything? Water? Coffee? Juice? A cab?"

"So you think this is funny? You think this is some kinda joke?"

Carpious sits opposite Alethea in an oversized, brown leather chair diagonal to the couch. A glass table that runs parallel and about three-quarters the length of the couch divides them. Atop the table is a remote control; an empty, ornate vase; and four magazines neatly fanned out to reveal the titles—*Forbes*, *Newsweek*, *Fortune*, and *Financial Times*—the last of which is some religious or financial trade magazine.

"I'm not joking, Alethea," Carpious says without a glint of a smile. "I want to resolve this idea that I owe you anything for once and for all. I've gone on with my life. You need to do the same. *Without* bothering me."

"So you gon' just let me die? You gon' act like you never loved me?" Alethea's voice trembles.

Carpious stares in her direction and displays no emotion as he waits for the next part of her seeming act.

"It wasn't that long ago you was in prison writing me letters about how much you *loved* me. Remember? Remember we met online while you was in prison finishing up a twenty year piece for murder? Murder. You didn't do the whole twenty because you was going to school and volunteering and trusting in God and shit."

Carpious says nothing but continues to stare.

"They ended up letting you out after twelve and you had finished up most of your degree. Remember? We got married right after you got out and the preacher—what was his name?"

Alethea looks to the side and frowns as she tries to recall for a long silent minute. Suddenly she springs back to life and bounces in her seat snapping her fingers, excited at her point of recall. "Moser! Rosco? Rusty? Russell! Russell Moser! That was his name. He married us and helped you get a job. Remember? Yeah, we was in love and I remember you was studying for some big test that you had to take when you got that job. I was there for you the *whole* time. Supporting *yo'* ass! And now you act like you can't remember none o' that shit?"

Carpious frowns. "Alethea, I *do* remember. But who I *was* is *not* who I am. Yeah, I was in prison. I got caught up in something as a kid. But you know what? I grew up. I made that right. I made something of myself. And I thought you were going to do the same. I thought you were leaving your past behind too. But this history lesson you just gave me is just a reminder that you haven't changed anything but your clothes—if that."

Alethea rises from her seat but pauses. She starts shaking her head and sits back down. "Nah. I'm gon' let that one go, you cold-hearted motherfucka. I got AIDS and you makin' jokes 'bout it. Okay. But I was there fo' you. And you left me as soon as you got out. Left me down and out. My heart was broke, Carpious. I was crushed. All the time you was in jail, I was visiting you and writing you and encouraging you and shit. I was there fo' you!"

"You were there for me, Alethea? All the time we were corresponding, you failed to tell me that you had a drug problem. All that I married—all that I thought you were—was a lie. I was busy trying to get my life together and you were busy getting high."

"So I'm not perfect. Who are *you*, Mr. Goody Two Shoes? Is the glory of God shining outta yo' ass crack? I been tryin' to get myself together. When you left me, I was crushed…" Alethea's voice crackles on the verge of tears and she pauses for a moment.

Then she continues, more composed and calm, "My heart…I just wanted to be loved. So the first smilin' Jim that came along, I didn't look twice. I didn't ask questions. I didn't even care. I just wanted to be loved. I accepted whateva… just to be loved. He put his hands on me twice and I didn't see reason to leave even then. I was blind until I found out he gave me AIDS. He knew he had it when he met me and didn't even tell me—"

Carpious interrupts, "I'm sorry you got hurt. I really am. But you made that choice. Not me. You can't blame me for what *you* got yourself into."

Alethea stands up again pointing at Carpious. "You a fine one to talk, Carpious. You a fine one to try and judge *me*. I never hurt nobody gettin' high. I never killed nobody gettin' high. But you…Mr. Pious Almighty walk around like stank don't blow from yo' fuckin' shit!"

"Alethea, lest you forget, this *is* my home. You *will* sit down and show me some respect or you *will* leave."

Alethea holds her arms rigid with fists clenched and frowns while mocking a deep voice, "Lest you forget, blah blah blah. Motherfucka, please. You started that shit. Ain't nobody disrespectin' you."

Alethea sits back down. Carpious sits up from his relaxed posture and weighs in more intently. "This showing up at my house *uninvited* is disrespectful. I've heard all that I'm going to hear at this point. You have nothing more to say to me."

"I already told you what I gotta say. You just ain't listenin'. I just got out of rehab. The little job I got ain't paying a lot, so I can't afford the medicine they got me on. I already applied for assistance but that's not enough to live on. It's like if you in the system relying on they shit, they take care of you, but if you tryin' to make it on yo' own, they make it impossible."

"You sing that sad song to someone else, Alethea! I made it out. You can too."

"You had help, motherfucka! That preacher. The warden. Me! You forget. You didn't pull yo'self up on yo' own. And soon as you make it, you forget about everybody else. You turn into a sellout motherfucka."

Carpious stands up. "I've been patient for long enough. That's enough. You're going to have to leave."

"Oh! You can't handle the truth about yourself, I see. You done so much to hide who you are and where you come from. I bet yo' girlfriend and yo' neighbors don't even know who you really are. And you gon' raise up on a sistah? Motherfucka, please. Why don't I give that light-eyed, curly bitch of yo's a phone call? I'm sure she don't know her man is an ex-con still connin'."

Carpious walks over to Alethea and reaches for her arm. "Come on. Get out."

She slaps his hand away. "I will fuck you up! Put your hand on me again!"

Carpious sighs and looks at Alethea. "Alethea, I'm not playing this game anymore. I'm not responsible for you. I'm not paying you any money. Do you want to know why? Because you would smoke it up and come back for more later and the cycle would never stop. I'm not going to enable you. You're on your own. Be a woman and do something for yourself for a change."

Alethea looks silent and defeated. Carpious looms over her, waiting for some kind of response.

"I guess I won't be the only one who knows about you then. You pay or I say."

"What? Are you *really* serious? You're really going to try and blackmail me?" Carpious exclaims.

He walks out of the living room. Alethea remains seated but nervously looks around to see where Carpious has gone. She prepares herself for anything.

Except...

The sound of Carpious' fearful voice on the phone in another room says, "Yes, I'm calling to report a break-in in progress at my residence. No, no one is hurt, but I'm afraid that I may be in danger. I think the intruder has a weapon. Yes, that's the correct address. Yes, I am locked in another room to avoid confrontation. The intruder may hear me talking to you. Please hurry."

Alethea hears Carpious hang the phone up. He returns from around the corner. "Alethea, leave my home now or I will attach a name to that intruder. Come here again and I will have you arrested."

Alethea stands and faces Carpious in disbelief. "You piece of shit!"

Carpious smiles.

"See? Once a con, always a con. This whole life of yours that you have now is a con."

Carpious scoffs while looking away and then turns to face Alethea. He leans in over her with a serious look on his face and his hands stuffed in his pockets. "Well at least it's my life. What do *you* have?"

He steps back and pulls his left hand from his pocket to scratch the side of his nose with his thumb. He leans in again with an arrogant smirk. "Oh...that's right. AIDS. *That's* what you got."

Alethea mouths, "Motherfuck..." before exploding into a tantrum, flailing her fists at Carpious.

He reacts, yanking his head sideways and backward putting his unpocketed hand in front of Alethea to prevent her advance. Her wild fit penetrates Carpious' defense and she grabs the lapel of his shirt with one hand. Carpious jerks his other hand out of his pocket and with it he shoves Alethea from him. His strength and size are more than enough to fling her backward like a discarded sheet of paper. She lands backward on the couch

"Stop it!" Carpious barks at Alethea as if she is a disobedient pet who has just soiled the carpet.

Alethea kicks to recover from her fall, and for a moment, she resembles a turtle trapped on its back. She springs up, but Carpious has already made his way toward the front door. He flings the door open to dismiss his unwelcome guest. "Get out n—"

Something explodes against the door inches from Carpious' head. He jerks away from the deafening sound and looks in Alethea's direction. She has just thrown the ceramic vase that was sitting on the coffee table at him. Suddenly, pain stings the side of his face. He raises his hand to feel the wetness of blood and grit. His eyes widen at the realization that shrapnel from the vase has cut the left side of his face. He looks toward Alethea with a snarl of hatred and violent intent. His fists clench and his body turns rigid. New and sudden fear backs Alethea behind the chair that Carpious was previously sitting in.

"You stupid cunt. You want to see me. You want to see who I was? You're dead. I told you to leave and—"

Red and blue strobe lights dance on Carpious' bloodied face at the moment his rage decides upon advancing in Alethea's direction. He jerks around to see the police car that has pulled into his driveway. Two officers are already out of the car and approaching the porch. He walks out to meet them. One of the officers walks past Carpious into the house. The other addresses Carpious.

"Sir, do you need an ambulance? Are you okay?"

Carpious feigns fear. "She's inside. I-It's my ex-wife. I opened the door and she just barged in a-and attacked me. I wish to press charges."

"*The mass of men lead lives of quiet desperation. What is called resignation is confirmed desperation.*"

– Henry David Thoreau

CHAPTER EIGHT

Time. It's just something one wears on his wrist. An artificial structure. A figment. A representative. Like the lines that divide states or countries on a map, those lines are not really there. Time has been said to "heal all wounds," but in reality, time doesn't heal anything. It simply passes, while the pain, loss, or trauma and how a person deals with it determines whether he is healed or is worse off than before

Three weeks have passed since Carpious' contretemps with Alethea. His facial wounds have healed into scars that are only apparent because of his light-hued skin. He hasn't heard from Alethea since the incident and assumes that she's still in jail for assault since it's unlikely that she could afford to post bail. His physical scars are little more than a reminder that the passage of time is delaying the healing of a wound that may indeed be festering inside.

Bernie Loomis' home has the lingering odor of moth balls or mildew that has been overcome by the fragrance of cinnamon and citrus. The air is hot and moist as if the thermostat was set to eighty degrees on a rainy day. Artificial light competes with the rare February hint of sunlight as the curtains are open to allow the energy of the world inside.

Carpious sits at a table in Bernie's kitchen as his sixty-three-year-old neighbor and friend sorts through cabinets in search of matching drinking glasses.

"You can't drink Scotch from a tumbler. It just ain't right. I know...I know I have another glass in here somewhere," Bernie breathes heavily from exertion.

Carpious interrupts, "Do you need me to help look? Or I can just go across the street and grab a couple of glasses."

Bernie peers up at Carpious from a cabinet that he's halfway into.

"You're my guest! I've been trying...to get you to sit and h-have a drink with me since...you moved into this neighborhood. You sit tight, young blood. I'll find that...other glass."

"You sound like you're out of breath there, Bern. I was just trying to be helpful."

"I'm not out of breath. I'm just...doing deep breathing...exercises. Ah! Found it."

Bernie holds up the thick, jeweled glass before turning to the sink to rinse it. He speaks louder over the running water. "Grab that bottle of Scotch in front of you. We're going to the sunroom."

Carpious stands and takes the brown bottle with the black and gold label that had been sitting in front of him. He politely waits for Bernie to finish drying the glasses to escort him out of the kitchen into the sunroom.

Bernie turns and sees Carpious waiting for him.

"Oh, you're waiting for me? I'm coming. I'm coming."

Bernie chuckles to himself as he walks past Carpious into the room adjacent to the kitchen. Carpious follows.

The room is spacious, white, and vacant of furniture, but there are lush and healthy green plants along the walls and covering most of the floor space. Bernie leads Carpious along a narrow trail around the greenery to the far side of the room replete with a wall of windows and two plush chairs with a small table between them. At the base of the table is a basket with assorted newspapers, magazines, and books. The high-backed chairs face into the room instead of looking outside. Bernie plops down in the chair on the right, as this is assuredly the one he usually occupies, while Carpious sits in its less-worn ally.

Bernie reaches for the bottle of Scotch and Carpious resigns it to him. He pours a half serving in each glass and hands one of the glasses to Carpious. Bernie raises his glass and nods to Carpious who does the same.

"Cheers," Bernie smiles.

"Cheers," Carpious echoes as their glasses clink.

Carpious cautiously sips while Bernie takes a large gulp and sits back baring his teeth as he lets out a satisfied sigh. Bernie glances over to Carpious whose lips are barely touching the upturned glass.

"Would you like a straw with that, young blood?" he asks before exploding into laughter.

"This is my very first Scotch experience. I'm savoring every flavor," Carpious rasps.

"Well, be careful with it. The heat doesn't hit you until *after* you swallow it. Conversation, Scotch, and a good friend—I can think of no better way to spend my Saturday afternoon. There have been times in the past where I had such rough days with clients that I dreamed of reaching in my jacket pocket for a flask and taking a swig right in front of the bosses in the middle of a meeting."

Carpious chuckles with a deep voice and Bernie joins in with a cackle that makes his whole body shake.

"Yeah. That would make your client calls *very* interesting."

"So Bernie, what exactly *do* you do with your days lately? Aren't you retired now?"

"No, I'm not retired *yet*. My days are still pretty busy, seems like things won't be slowing down anytime soon. I could retire and collect Social Security benefits now, you know, but I plan on staying on the job a couple more years so that I can hang on to my health insurance benefits, which are so much better than Medicare."

Bernie pauses to think for a moment and then continues. "Ida and I were planning on retiring together and traveling, you know. I think I'll still do that. I've earned it, sitting at a desk for twenty-eight years, processing loans and managing an office, training people. I love what I do—helping people realize their dreams—but I've earned a real vacation, you know."

"I assumed you were retired, but I guess never really thought about what you did on a daily basis. Processing loans?"

"Yep. I'm in the same business as you—money. *You* deal with the big corporations and *I* deal with the average Joe's small business and commercial property."

"That's interesting. I can't picture you at a desk. You seem like you have to always be moving. Are you looking forward to retirement? I wonder what most people do all day after they retire."

"When Ida was alive we joked about how we were going to spend retirement playing pranks on working stiffs. You know when you get old you're entitled to do that without penalty. People expect you to be solemn, so it really throws them off when you act just as young and mischievous as they are. The benefits of being old."

Carpious laughs, "I guess so."

"There was this joke I heard once...let me see, how did it go? Um...okay okay. I remember now."

Bernie continues in character, "The other day, my wife and I went into town and went to this shop. We were only there for about five minutes, and when we came out, there was a cop writing out a parking ticket. We went up to him and said, 'Come on, officer...how about giving a senior citizen a break?' He ignored us and continued writing the ticket, so then I started calling him names. He glared at me and wrote another ticket for having worn tires, so then my wife joins in and called him some more names. He finished the second ticket and put it on the windshield with the first. Then he started writing a third ticket. This went on for about twenty minutes. The more we abused him, the more tickets he wrote. Personally, we didn't care. It wasn't our car. We came into town by bus."

Bernie and Carpious explode into laughter and continue on for about two minutes before trailing off. Bernie refills both of their glasses and sits back with a sigh and a melancholy smile on his face. Carpious sits quietly, waiting for him to say more.

"Yes, I sure do miss Ida. That woman had a fierce sense of humor. I could see us as that crazy couple."

Bernie takes a swallow while looking straight ahead longingly reminiscing. Carpious respectfully remains quiet.

"How long were you married, Carpious?"

Carpious is stunned by the blunt question but recovers quickly. "Umm, just two years," he answers in brief, not volunteering anything else.

"What happened? Why'd you get divorced?" Bernie probes.

"Well...I met Alethea—her name is Alethea—I met her at a time in my life when I was...transitioning. I was in a different place then. When we got married, I changed from the bitter man I'd become. I found out that she wasn't who she claimed to be; who she *really* was, was a danger to my growth. I had to grow and she wasn't willing to grow with me, so she had to go."

Carpious looks down at his empty glass and rolls it in between his palms in silence.

"I see. Was that her too?" Bernie asks pointing at the left side of Carpious' face.

Carpious raises a hand to touch his face as if he'd forgotten the scars there.

"Oh...yes. She came around wanting to get back to-gether but I told her that I've moved on with my life. She got furious when I wouldn't succumb to her advances and threw a glass at me. She missed me, but the glass hit the door and some of the shards cut my face." Carpious makes deliberate eye contact with Bernie and says with a serious look, "I'm sorry for the ruckus that night. I'm certain she won't be back though."

"You seem to be so calm and handle conflict well. Was that from military training?"

"Military?"

"Yeah. You seem like the military type. I know I make a lot of assumptions, but you've only been in finance a few years and you come across as so...uh...together. I thought you were previously in the military or perhaps your folks were. Am I wrong?"

"No. You got me. Guilty as charged." Carpious raises his hands in mock surrender.

Bernie laughs. "Devil dog, squid, airman, or Joe?"

"Er… huh? What do you mean?"

"What branch of the military were you in?"

"Oh. Sorry… Army. Yeah. Eight years."

"Okay. I can see that. I'm not sure if it's your personality or what you've found to be a habit, but you seem like the leader type—the kind to confront the issue and get things done."

"Well thanks, Bernie. I'm not sure if that's the way it really is, but they say that perception is more reality than reality."

Bernie laughs again and Carpious joins in. Bernie's blithe expression suddenly falters to a stern silence as if he's struggling to think of something. He then turns to Carpious.

"Have you met the guy who bought 361?"

Carpious nods his head in the direction of 361 Mechi Lane. "You mean up the street in the cul-de-sac? No. I know that someone moved in a month or so ago, but I've not seen him. He's done a good job of making himself scarce. Maybe he travels a lot with his job. Have you met him?"

"No, and I'm not sure what he does, but I *do* know what he *did*."

Carpious frowns, confused.

"What? What do you mean?"

"How often do you check your mail?"

"How often do I…? What? What are you…?"

"When was the *last* time you checked your mail?"

"Last weekend, I suppose. I usually just get junk mail so I don't check it everyday. Why?"

"If you were to check your mail today, it's likely that you have the same letter that I got two days ago. I'll show it to you. Hold on."

Bernie grunts as he thrusts himself out of his chair. He places his empty glass on the table between the chairs and leaves the room. Carpious' confused expression remains. He lifts his glass to his mouth and tosses back the remaining contents. Bernie returns as quickly as he left holding an envelope. As he sits back down, he unfolds a piece of paper and hands it to Carpious. Carpious sits back in the chair to let the light fall on the typed form letter.

Bernie studies Carpious intently while he reads the letter. Carpious shows little concern or emotion as his eyes dart back and forth across the paper.

It reads:

Dear Neighbors,

It has come to my attention that the new owner and occupant of 361 Mechi Lane, Ian Kaplan, is registered with the city of Admah City as a sex offender. His previous crime was statutory rape. Now, while I don't know the details of his conviction, I ask that we remain accountable and watchful of our children on Mechi Lane.

The intent of this letter is not to organize a witch hunt but to draw us into a greater sense of vigilance, as a neighborhood and an extended family. Thank you for your prompt attention.

Sincerely,

Amril Flores
HOA Secretary

Carpious looks at Bernie as he sits up to return the letter to him. He searches Bernie's face for some type of response.

"We need *you* to talk to this guy, Carpious."

"Me? Why?"

"Just like I've said a million times, everybody loves you. You have a way with people. There's an intensity about you that would show this...this pedophile not to try any funny business around here. You're both a teddy bear and a grizzly bear. You could feel him out and use intimidation, if necessary, to get your point across."

"Uh... Bernie...I don't think that I—"

"Most of the people who live here have kids; think of *them* Carpious."

"We don't know that this guy is a danger to anyone. How long ago was he convicted? He could be different now."

Bernie hears the doubtful tone in Carpious' voice as he tries to wriggle free of the task being bestowed on him. "People like that don't change! He's sick, and somehow the system has let this sicko buy a house here. We need to let him know that this will not be his playground. Will you talk to him? At least feel him out? See where his head is?"

"Keep your friends close but your enemies closer?"

"Exactly! I've talked to a couple of other people and they agree that you should talk to him."

"Oh, I've been drafted by the council of the neighborhood, huh?"

"Well, as the newly elected president of the Home Owners Association of Mechi Lane..."

"Okay, okay. I'll talk to him."

"Thank you, Carpious. You're one of the few good guys left."

Carpious awkwardly smiles as the languor of alcohol settles in.

~

What drives someone to wear the cowl of the recluse, hermit, loner, or pariah? What nagging root persists that community—the constant presence of people—is not as desirable as solitude? Is it circumstance or choice?

For Ian Kaplan, it is both. He has recently spent his days in seclusion unpacking boxes, moving furniture, planning, and painting. Considering that Ian was born to wealth, this is perhaps the most work he's done in his entire life. His father is a prosperous real estate mogul who has distanced himself from Ian relationally but still provides for Ian financially, as long as he keeps his distance from the family and stays out of trouble. His own family pays him to stay away from them—that fact alone could make *any* man an emotional recluse.

Suddenly, a sound Ian has not heard in the two months he's been at 361 Mechi Lane interrupts his thoughts. The deliberate and authoritative knock startles him.

"Who…who is it?" he mumbles as he jumps up from his recliner. He draws a curtain back to see a man standing on his porch, waiting.

"Who is it?" Ian repeats louder.

"Carpious, your neighbor down the street. I just wanted to say hello and introduce myself."

"Just a minute."

Ian takes a deep breath and glances around his home before turning the latch on two deadbolts to open the front door.

Ian opens the door to see Carpious smiling back at him. Carpious fills the doorway and towers over Ian's five-foot-nine-inch, gangly build.

"Hello," Carpious begins, "I live at 163 on the corner."

Ian peers back, squinting, and says nothing.

Carpious fills the awkward void by repeating, "Hello? I'm your neighbor up the—"

"I know you," Ian finally says as he swings the door wide open, his mouth agape.

"Excuse me?" Carpious responds, confused.

"I never forget a face. I know *yours*."

"Uhhh…okay?"

"No, I mean I know *of* you."

"You must have me confused wi—"

"You saved me."

"W-what? Saved you? We've never met."

"No, we've never met *personally*. But I *know* you."

Carpious stares back at Ian as if he's beginning to question his lucidity.

"I-I know that doesn't make sense. Let me explain. I know you from your name and I've seen you before. A long while ago, but I will never forget you. They started calling you Pious Almighty after you killed Herc."

Carpious' eyes widen before he tries to smile off the shock. "You definitely have me confused with someone else."

"No. No, I don't. I never forget a face, especially the face of the man who was responsible for repeatedly raping me in prison. I can never forget his face either. You killed him. You saved me."

Carpious continues to be stunned as he suddenly becomes aware of his surroundings. He nervously looks around.

"Umm…Ian…can I…" Carpious takes another deep breath. "May I come inside?"

Ian steps back. "Please, do come in."

CHAPTER NINE

Lela Janson is crying. For the past nine months, Lela Janson has been crying for sundry reasons; hormonal sensitivity, fear, internal conflict, happiness, or whatever biological reaction accompanies the overabundance of estrogen. Today, Lela Janson is crying because she is in immense pain. Today, Lela is having a baby.

Her husband, Drew, sits by her bedside in an awkward, wooden chair with pleather backing and seating. He shifts his weight every two minutes but the slippery, faux leather won't let him sit comfortably. The lack of décor in the Janson's private room at Mercy General Hospital is not promoting tranquility. The eggshell-colored walls feature two small paintings that have little to do with childbirth. One scene features flowers of magenta, green, and faded yellow spilling out of a vase in the center of the frame. The other, which is more abstract in nature, is predominately brown and textured with a giant swath, a stroke of royal blue, drawn diagonally and stretching from the middle of the painting to the bottom. A nineteen-inch flat-screen television is mounted on the wall across from Lela's bed and Drew has it resting on a news channel but the volume is down. Lela has quieted her crying to a whine and is leaning sideways out of the bed, gripping the edges with her fingers.

"Drew…I think I need the epidural shot. I can't take anymore. Go get the nurse."

Drew stands to attention.

"Okay. Are you sure? Is it too late now? To get the shot? Are you sure you—"

"Drew…please…don't play doctor. Go get the nurse," Lela whimpers between contractions.

"Let me turn the television to a music channel with something more calming. You don't want to watch this depressing news crap."

Drew fidgets with the remote pointing it at the wall. Apparently the batteries are weak because he presses the remote repeatedly and the television doesn't respond. After a few long seconds pass and he has found a classical station, he turns his attention to Lela who has abandoned her pleas for him to find a nurse.

"Come hold me," Lela whines, now curled on her side.

Drew sits on the side of the bed and leans in to comfort his wife. The bed is too small to accommodate them both, so his embrace is more of a presence than anything more intimate. He rocks his weight back and forth to lull her into some semblance of calm. Chopin's "Prelude in D Flat" plays in the background as a soundtrack to accompany Lela's moaning.

After a few moments of stillness, Drew stirs. "Baby, I'm going to call Carpious and check on Haleigh. I'll be right back."

"What? Why do you have to leave to call?"

"You need your rest and I don't want to disturb you.

I'll be right back."

He's already started toward the door.

"Dreeeew…don't leeeeeave," Lela calls, but the door is already swinging closed following Drew's abrupt exit.

The hallway is a bustle of people holding clipboards, wearing lab coats and scrubs, or attending to patients in rolling beds or wheelchairs. Drew occupies a spot close to the wall out of the way of traffic so as to not interrupt the activity of the nurses, doctors, and patients. He holds his cell phone to the side of his face while looking down at the white linoleum floor. He paces back and forth with one hand in his pocket, waiting for someone to answer on the other end.

"Hello?" a voice greets after the fourth ring.

"Hello? Carpious?"

"Hello, Drew."

"Hey! How's Haleigh?"

"Oh, we're doing great over here. The whole gang is here. Haleigh is playing with Solomon and Sydney and I are preparing dinner. But you know Haleigh is always great. No worries at all. More importantly, how is Lela? Has she had the baby yet?"

"No, not yet. The baby is going to come when the baby is ready, you know." Drew sighs.

"You sound a little frustrated there, Drew. Are *you* okay?"

"Oh, I'm fine. It's just…we've been here for two nights now, Carpious. I guess I'm just nervous and ready for the baby to come."

"Well, I'm praying for Lela, that she'll be fine and the baby will be fine. Don't worry. You'll be a dad again before you know it. Tell that wife of yours that we're thinking about her and everything is okay."

"Okay. Thanks, Carpious. We appreciate you. Hey! Can I speak to Haleigh right quick? She's been crying a lot lately and I just want to make sure she's feeling alright."

"I am proud to report that there have been no tears here. Hold on a second, let me get her."

Seconds pass as Drew waits for his daughter to come to the phone. He paces past the nurse who has been attending his wife but barely notices her as his focus is elsewhere. He hears scuffling on the other end of the phone.

"Hello," Haleigh answers.

"Hey, sweetie."

"Hi, Daddy."

"Sweetie, I just wanted to hear your voice and tell you that I love you. Okay?"

"Okay. Do I have a little brother yet?"

"Not yet, but we're working on it, okay?"

"Okay, Daddy."

"Are you having fun with Mr. Carpious? Haleigh?"

"Drew?" Carpious' voice returns on the other end.

"Hey. What happened?"

"Haleigh just gave the phone back to me. Seven-year olds, you know."

"Yeah. Don't I know it."

"Well, get back to your wife and know that all is well on this end. Keep us posted."

"Okay. Thanks, Carpious."

"No problem. Bye now."

Drew slides the phone from his face and snaps it shut taking a deep breath. Once again, he checks his surroundings and opens the phone to make another call. He walks further away from his wife's room and doesn't see that two nurses enter.

"Hey…it's me," he whispers into the phone he's holding to the side of his face again.

~

As Carpious prepares lunch in his kitchen, the vocal elation of Haleigh and Solomon playing in the front yard on a sunny day wafts in and lingers throughout the house. Carpious has opened most of the windows to welcome the pleasant breeze and smells of spring. Sydney, assisting by Carpious' side, quietly smiles as her thoughts have surely been reflecting on innocence. Carpious is quiet too, but his focus seems to be on artfully cutting finger-sized wedges from folds of turkey and melted cheese snuggled between slices of bread.

"I'm so excited for Lela," Sydney gushes. "I can't wait until she delivers and I get a chance to hold and smell a newborn baby again!"

Carpious and Sydney look up at each other at the same time. She pauses while cutting the fruit to chuckle. "No, no, no. I'm perfectly fine with holding someone else's baby. Don't you worry, mister," Sydney laughs.

Carpious smiles and resumes cutting sandwiches.

Sydney continues, "When I was in labor with Solomon, his dad was already gone. I was so scared. I mean, my mom was there and all, but, Lela is fortunate to have Drew right there, you know?"

Carpious scoffs under his breath.

Sydney pauses again and turns to face Carpious.

"What? I know that sound, Mr. Mightson. What is it?"

"Nothing. Nothing at all. I'm just saying. Lela is fortunate to have great friends like *us*."

"Sure. That's not what you meant and you know it. Have your little secrets then. You know, the woman *always* finds out," Sydney teases.

Carpious smiles outwardly but clearly his thoughts are elsewhere. Neither Sydney's playfulness nor the sound of the kids playing in the yard has swayed his mood. He remains unaffected…and elsewhere.

~

Rhoda Mightson was a strict woman who expected much of her only son, Carpious. Her constant attention and nurturing discipline forced him to become a child whose innate maturity was betrayed by his childish size. Carpious was often compelled, due to his mother's strict nature, to idolize his father who was an absentee parent. During times of frustration with his mother's incessant attention, he fantasized about what life would be like under his father's supervision instead.

In the early spring of his eleventh year, Carpious found out that his fantasies would soon become a reality. His mother had been diagnosed with an aggressive strain of leukemia. She'd already been receiving chemotherapy, but the treatments were only delaying the inevitable; she was dying.

Rhoda initiated a dialogue with Carpious' father, Benjamin Mightson, at the onset of her cancer, in hopes that he would give evidence of a desire to be an integral part of Carpious' life. In the event of her demise, Rhoda wanted to secure Carpious' future, and she knew he worshipped his father.

His mother died in late winter the year Carpious turned twelve. As previously orchestrated, his father took custody and Carpious couldn't have been happier. Though he was forlorn at the death of his mother, Carpious felt vindicated with his father there. He felt that he could express himself freely and be understood. Though his father had been a stranger to him previously, he felt that he knew him as well as he knew his own reflection in the mirror. Carpious' ideological view of his father prevented him from seeing the true Benjamin Mightson, the abusive, alcoholic, disgrace of a parent that he really was and would prove to be.

One night Carpious' father reached a point of intoxication that led him to cross a heinous line and commit an irreparable offense; he sexually molested Carpious.

What greater rancor has a man than sexually abusing a child? What callous, vile, malicious act could be worse? In those blinding moments, the man whom young Carpious equated to God—the man that he thought bigger than God—betrayed him.

That unforgivable assault happened again, and again, until Carpious was numb. The only feeling he was capable of feeling was rage. He would have been better off not knowing this stranger who once seemed to be his Superman. Admiration had eroded to hatred and all Carpious wanted was for his rage to be extinguished; and one fateful day, it was.

The local newspaper announced to the world what would happen no more:

ADMAH CITY — On May 11, Benjamin Carpious Mightson Sr. was shot by his 12-year-old son with a small caliber handgun. Mightson was shot in the face but survived the assault and is in stable condition at Mercy General Hospital. Authorities say that the boy flew into a rage during an argument with his father before firing the gun, stolen from a secured location in the home. The boy attempted to fire the gun several times after it jammed. Neighbors called the police and discovered Mightson unconscious on the kitchen floor. The boy fled the scene but is now in custody.

Because he is a minor, the boy has been transferred to the Lyman State Continuation School for Boys. Neighbors are being questioned and have expressed shock at what has happened in their quiet neighborhood.

Charges have yet to be filed but are expected.

~

Carpious stares at the cutting board on the counter in front of him. Thoughts of his mother find him once again considering the destruction of innocence that his father's abrupt entry and exit caused. He recalls being disposed to legal custody of the state once found guilty of aggravated assault with a deadly weapon. He remembers the rumors of his insanity and all of the tests that followed.

Carpious never had contact, nor spoke to his father again, after the morning he shot him. After reconstructive surgery and several days in intensive care, his father survived the gunshot wound to the right eye. The small caliber bullet ricocheted in his sinus cavity and rendered him legally blind. Benjamin Carpious Mightson Sr. lived eight more years, suffering severe headaches and vertigo before dying of unrelated causes according to medical reports. Once in the penal system, life for Carpious only got worse—much worse.

Suddenly, Carpious is startled into the present by the gentle touch on his shoulder and Sydney's voice.

"Honey? Are you okay? Carpious?"

Carpious stirs to consciousness and turns to Sydney. "Oh...I was just, uh, lost in my head...remembering."

"Remembering what? By the look on your face, it must not have been a good memory."

Over the past few years, Carpious has learned to hide his emotion and physical expressions well. Rather than emote joy, anger, disgust, or whatever he may be feeling, it is easier to simply be consistently monotone or—as others would mistake to *his* advantage—calm, cool, and collected.

But Sydney caught him with his guard down in that moment, reflecting on the horror of his childhood. Within those few moments of exposure she saw a glimpse of something she had never gleaned from him before. She saw a stranger.

"What's going on with you, Carpious? Come on," Sydney probes.

Could he trust her? Could he tell her everything? Who he really was and where he came from? Would she be repulsed by all that he'd done? Or flinch at what had been done to him?

"I...the thought of childbirth...it just made me think about my own parents," Carpious fumbles as he smiles to mask his pain and strokes Sydney's shoulder.

He continues now conscious of himself and his expressions, "They died when I was young so I...I was just wondering what it would have been like if they were still around."

Sydney wraps her slender, dark arms around Carpious' torso and pulls herself so close that she has to crane her neck to look into his eyes.

"Oh, honey, I understand. Believe me. Daddy died when I was a teenager and I miss him too. He was a good man."

"A good man," Carpious thinks to himself. "What does that really look like?"

What would it feel like to completely come clean? Expose it all. Break down the façade of a life that he'd built...and not apologize for the broken pieces. Would full disclosure emancipate him? Would it give him the opportunity to be the man his father never was? Could that lead to forgiveness for himself, or his father?

"No! Never," Carpious shakes his head in silent response to the soliloquy echoing in his head.

~

Several hours of labor pains have ebbed, and Drew and Lela Janson are now both resting. Drew is sprawled across the pleather chair in the corner with a small blanket that covers only the top half of his body. Lela is lying motionless on her side with her mouth open. Hospital sheets and extra blankets cover her so that only her head peeks out from underneath. It's been a long and arduous day for her, but less than five feet away from her in a sterile bassinet lies the reward for her battle. Caleb Andrew Janson, born a mere three hours ago, is in perfect company among the sleeping. He slumbers swaddled in a light blue blanket dotted with green ducks and racecars.

The sun has retreated to a distant horizon and there is little activity in the hallway beyond the Janson's private room.

CHAPTER TEN

Resentment has the potential to consume many who appear to be otherwise blameless. Unresolved caged resentment that one day breaks free and kills all of the delicate innocence in the yard. Acidic, rancorous resentment has gears for teeth that are perfectly oiled by bitterness and possess a judgment unable to discern the corrupted from the good.

Twenty-seven years ago, an eighteen-year old boy provided a refuge and a home for that resentment. Twenty-seven years ago, an eighteen-year old young man gave birth to a hatred that was the illegitimate off-spring of resentment. Twenty-seven years ago, resent-ment changed Carpious Mightson and he died a death that no one was left to grieve for.

He'd been transferred to Siddim Valley State Prison following his seventeenth birthday, after spending three years of a four-year sentence for aggravated assault with a deadly weapon at Lyman State Continuation School for Boys. While at Lyman State, Carpious maintained a quiet demeanor and kept to himself. When he did *socialize*, it was often in the form of fighting with other boys, which earned him the wrong kind of attention from the authorities responsible for him. He was labeled a troublemaker and any consideration of releasing him into a foster home, to finish out his teenage years, was abandoned because of his erratic and violent outbursts, outbursts that commanded fear and kept others at a respective distance.

Prison is not reform school. The incarcerated at Siddim Valley State Prison were as young as sixteen and as mature as seventy-two. There was a climate of hopelessness throughout that infected even the correctional officers who simply worked there to support their families. Consistent order and routine was commanded on the surface, but corruption bled underneath like a hematoma bleeds into a contained area under skin. The trafficking of illegal contraband such as tobacco, marijuana, and cocaine was both a way for the authorities to regulate calm and for the various gangs to wage conflict with power. Carpious kept to himself and took no part in the exchange of drugs or struggle for power, but fear of his reserve was soon tested because, at Siddim Valley State Prison, everyone is in debt to something or someone.

Unless Siddim State was under lockdown and all privileges were revoked, which happened more often than not, prisoners had fifteen minutes before lights out to roam in the immediate vicinity of their cells under scrutiny of the correctional officers. On paper, this privilege was a reward to prisoners for good behavior, intended to promote morale that would reverse the ill effects of incarceration and discourage violent and criminal characteristics. In reality, this was a criminal's opportunity to pass contraband through channels, intimidate rivals, and find sexual release at the cost of weaker prisoners. Carpious was not reputed to be one of these weaker ones, but Dante "Herc" Graham had grown arrogant with the power that he'd acquired over others during his first twelve years of a life sentence for second-degree murder and rape.

Twenty-seven years ago, one night, and nine minutes before lockdown, Carpious' cell door was closed but was not to be locked for another eight minutes. He was reclined across the bottom bunk tending to a crossword puzzle book that was already filled out when Herc opened the cell door and leaned against the iron frame of the bars. Another man stood behind him outside the cell in the walkway.

Herc had a commanding presence at six foot four inches. He was a wide, chunky man who was more muscle than fat, and his skin was so dark that it had a bluish tinge to it under the fluorescent lights. His linebacker-sized arms were covered in a chaotic mess of black tattoos that would remind one of barbed wire. Like all of the other prisoners, he was dressed in an orange jumpsuit with short sleeves rolled over his biceps, giving his upper torso a squared appearance.

"Fuck you readin', homie?" Herc barked toward Carpious who glanced up from his book but then resumed tracing penciled words with his finger, saying nothing.

Herc's eyes widened at the perceived disrespect, and he straightened up fully in front of the doorframe. He looked behind him and nodded to the other prisoner standing guard as he stepped into Carpious' cell and shut the door. Carpious looked up again.

Herc continued, "Niggas 'fraid of you 'cause you act like you some crazy mute and shit but I ain't fucking scared of yo' bitch ass, nigga. Stand yo' ass up!"

Carpious locked eyes with Herc and slowly stood up from his bed while displaying no apparent fear. Herc looked around again before he moved in closer to loom over Carpious. He leaned one hand against the top bunk that was temporarily empty and leaned in close. He stunk of feces and musk.

"You got five seconds to turn yo' ass 'round. I'm 'bout to make you my bitch, nigga. You quiet now but yo' ass gone scream my name in a minute."

Carpious' jaw tightened in concert with his body turning rigid. He looked up at his aggressor with a silent screaming defiance.

"Fuck you looking at me like that, nigga!" Herc responded violently.

Herc suddenly swung his other hand toward Carpious' face and struck with a closed fist, temporarily stunning him. Before Carpious could react, Herc grabbed him by both shoulders to turn Carpious around so that Carpious' neck was against the top bunk. Using the weight of one of his arms to anchor and strangle Carpious, Herc grabbed the collar of Carpious' jumpsuit with his free hand and pulled it down Carpious' back with such force that the front buttons released. Carpious was struggling for air and consciousness as Herc unbuttoned the front of his own jumpsuit while looking around.

Amidst the force and the stench and nearly blacking out, Carpious was confronted with the memory of a similar scenario that he played a part in where his father did the same thing to him, time and time again with the same brutality. The man who he idolized took away his innocence and was roaming free while Carpious was locked away with animals and bitter recollections. Carpious never had the chance to tell his father how he hated him or how he wanted to kill him as many times as he was raped by him. He never had the opportunity to look his father in the eyes as he drained the lifeblood from him.

Suddenly, Carpious struggled against Herc's advances. He jutted an elbow backward into Herc's ribs, surprising him enough to release his hold for a moment—a moment long enough for Carpious to gain air and ferocity to fling Herc back against the cell door. The door was blocked by the weight of Herc and the rage and strength of Carpious who'd begun to punch wildly. Herc was dazed and obviously not accustomed to taking punches because of his size as he waved his thick arms in Carpious' direction to try to fend him off. The prisoner standing guard reached though the cell bars to assist Herc and tried to grab Carpious, but to no avail. He brandished a weapon from the inside waist of his jumpsuit and violently tapped Herc, who was pressed against the bars by his off-balance weight, on the shoulder.

"Herc, Herc!"

Herc responded as if the scenario had been rehearsed and took hold of a three-inch shard of filed metal taped to a toothbrush handle.

He thrust the shard in Carpious' direction. The shiv entered Carpious' left shoulder, but before Herc could withdraw and strike again, Carpious grabbed it and, with both hands and the force of his rage and the will to survive, he thrust the blade up into Herc's abdomen. Herc slid down the bars into a seated position and clutched his stomach, which was now gushing blood. Carpious continued to stab him—in the chest, in the face, in the arms, and in the legs. The prisoner who handed Herc the weapon ran to get a guard.

Carpious said nothing the whole time as he thrust the blade and Herc went limp. The abrupt and disturbing sound of metal entering flesh was more akin to a spoon falling into dirty dishwater over and over again.

Carpious fell backward and slid across the floor to the other side of the cell facing the lifeless and bloodied body of Herc. His heaving was so loud that he didn't hear the lockdown sirens blaring or the voices shouting from outside the cell. Carpious didn't hear anything in those moments. He just stared wide-eyed, breathing heavily. Then, as if a wave of consciousness rushed in, he lifted his hands before him and saw them covered in the blood of his victim. Blood was across from him. Blood was on the floor. Blood was all over him—red, red blood.

~

Red carnations greet Sydney Durden as she sits at the front desk on the fifth floor of Mercy General Hospital in front of a monitor checking the status on all of her patients before she signs out for the evening. From behind the bouquet, a young boy with a hat covering his brow inquires about the location of the intended recipient.

"Is there a Sydney Durden here? I have a delivery for her."

A woman standing next to Sydney answers before she can. "She's sitting right here, honey."

The delivery boy places the large bouquet on the desk and places a clipboard in front of Sydney. "I just need your signature here, ma'am."

Sydney stands to scribble her name while Esther, her coworker, leans in over her to see whom the delivery is from.

"Girrrrrl, if your man is trying to make my husband look bad, he's doing a good job. This is the third time this week. What'd you do to get that man so wide open?"

"Thank you," Sydney says to the delivery boy as she hands him his clipboard back. "Hold on a second." Sydney leans down behind the desk to open a drawer where her purse is. After fumbling about for a few seconds she stands and leans forward to hand the delivery boy a wad of bills.

"Thank you, ma'am," he smiles as he takes the tip and bows slightly before leaving.

Sydney beams as she studies the arrangement of carnations sprinkled with smaller, puffy green and yellow daisies.

"Esther, I think I love this man most because I *cannot* figure him out. Just when I think I see him, just when I think I have him figured out, he surprises me again. And I don't mean in a bad way."

"What kind of flowers are these?"

"Carnations. I remember when I was a little girl my mom loved them. My dad would always get them for her on payday. What's funny is that he couldn't afford roses so he would get red carnations instead. My mom grew to love them so that when he *could* afford roses, she preferred carnations. I love them too because they remind me of my mom. I told Carpious that story and he's just ran with it ever since."

"Mmm. I can *see* that," Esther smirks with her arms crossed.

Sydney reaches into the bouquet and retrieves a card. She walks from behind the desk before reading it.

"What you got there?" Esther inquires.

"The flowers are for everyone to see. This card is for *my* eyes only," Sydney taunts.

The card is plain white and textured with flourishes in the corners. The printed text reads:

> While your loving attitude
> is like a flame that lights the gloom
> I miss you and can't wait to see you soon.

Sydney reads the note several times as if she's studying it for clues. A few moments pass as she slowly walks away to fully enjoy the sentiment with some degree of privacy. Suddenly, she holds the note to her chest and exclaims, "'In a Sentimental Mood' by Duke Ellington and John Coltrane!"

"What?" Esther asks as Sydney is walking back toward her.

"Oh. Carpious always leaves lyrics to a song that is both a personal note and a riddle for me. I always have to guess the song. This one is from a song called 'In a Sentimental Mood.'"

"Awww, suki suki now. I know that song. Bill and I made two of our kids listening to *that* song."

Sydney and Esther laugh as two more of their co-workers approach to marvel at the bouquet.

"Somebody *loves* somebody," one of them teases.

~

The evening sun gently warms Lela Janson's face as she sits on her porch and rocks back and forth in the swing, lulling Caleb to sleep on her shoulder as Haleigh sleeps in her lap. Her busy day of changing diapers and mending boo-boos is coming to an end, and while she is more exhausted than her two children, she can't run out of energy until they do. She waits, hoping that Drew will come to relieve her soon so that she too can rest. She waits hopeful.

~

Two hours pass and instead of relieving his wife at home, Drew is working late again to deliver a beta patch for software that his IT firm, AnalogDigits, released a month ago. As a project manager, Drew supervises a team of developers who've been frantically rewriting and testing code to reach an aggressive deadline. Last month, AnalogDigits released a package prematurely, causing a few clients to lose vital data with the upgrade. With the demands of being a new father, marital problems, and now standing in the crosshairs of angry bosses, Drew is stressed. Forgetfulness has always been an attribute of his, but lately it's gotten increasingly worse, much to Lela's disappointment. Tonight, he remembers that he was supposed to be home to relieve her of baby duty, albeit a few hours late.

Drew's office is a mess of stacks of papers on a desk with books lining the wall behind him. The only personal effects are an old picture of him, Lela, and Haleigh from about two years ago on his desk and a framed degree or certification hanging on the wall. Otherwise, the office is small and impersonal. Drew sits at his desk staring into two LCD computer monitors with a furrowed brow. He's holding his cell phone as if he's about to make a phone call, but he is interrupted as he looks at the chair opposite his desk that is usually occupied by a complaining employee afraid of losing her job.

And like clockwork, in walks the complaining and buxom Audrey Santello. Audrey is a beautiful woman with dark curly hair and olive skin. She toggles between being at an advantage working in a male-dominated environment and not being taken seriously because of her looks. A tiny voice that sounds like a twelve-year-old girl's doesn't help her case much in the way of being taken seriously by her male counterparts. Audrey is an intelligent and competent developer but she seems to always have something going on in her personal life that she has to complain to Drew about. Drew often complies with being a listening ear, which doesn't help Audrey too well in distinguishing boundaries between work and personal matters.

"Drew, are we going to get out of here soon?" Audrey whines in her nasally, high-pitched Spanish accent. "My mother is bitching about keeping my son and I don't want to hear it anymore. It's not like I don't give her money or anything. I can't *wait* to move out of there, man."

Audrey smells like a flowery perfume accident as she plops down in the chair. Her low-cut blouse is stuffed with breasts that jiggle to escape but settle down after a few moments. Drew struggles with whether he, as a man, can tell a woman who works for him that she needs to *not* wear so much perfume. He simply tolerates it. Often times, Audrey's fragrance lingers on his clothes hours after he's left work.

Drew stammers, "Well, Audrey, we're waiting for the, uh, files to propagate on the servers to make sure that there are no problems. As soon as Phil and Ashir give the thumbs up, we can all sing hallelujah and hopefully get out of here."

Audrey looks dissatisfied with Drew's answer but he holds up his cell phone and says, "Would you excuse me for a moment?"

Audrey leaves the room without saying a word, but her scent lingers loudly as Drew calls Lela.

"Lela, I'm going to be late tonight. I'm sorry I'm just getting around to calling," Drew mumbles into the phone.

"I figured that out two hours ago, Drew. I already put the kids down, so I'm going to bed. Caleb should be waking up again to eat soon. When will you be home?"

A man enters Drew's office smiling politely and quietly closes the door behind him.

"Uh...I *want* to say that I'm on my way, but I have to make sure that there are no more fires to put out since we uploaded the patch to the servers. I'll be on my way in about an hour if nothing goes wrong."

Lela, too tired to protest, simply sighs, "Okay, Drew."

"I'll be home as soon as I can."

With a mild look of concern, Drew slips his cell phone into his pocket as he stands to address the man still standing.

"What's up, Tony?"

Drew comes from around his desk.

"Calm down, Drew. Nothing's wrong. The files posted and tested fine. Phil is on the phone confirming everything. The nightmare is over. Everything's all set. Wanna go out to celebrate?"

"Ahh...I can't. This project has taken all of my free time. I need to get home to take care of Caleb."

"Isn't your wife home? The baby's probably asleep anyway. Come on. Just a drink or two?"

"Yeah, Lela's home—exactly where I need to be, Tone. I can't do this right now. I need to take some time off until things cool down at home. It's been too crazy all over for the past couple of months."

Tony moves closer to Drew and gently takes his hand looking him in the eye. "How are you going to take time off from who you really are, Drew? When are you going tell her about us? What are you waiting for? Come out of the closet, already."

Tony exhales sharply and continues, "You can only wear one face, Drew."

CHAPTER ELEVEN

His car pulls to an abrupt stop and before the turn of the key in the ignition can disengage the engine, Carpious bursts out of his vehicle. It's raining, as it has been for several days, and he steps into a large puddle of water as he stomps to where his ex-wife is standing. She's waiting on his front porch like before and she's drenched, wearing a look of desperation on her face. She flicks away a half-smoked cigarette as Carpious lumbers toward her.

"What are you doing here?" his voice booms synonymous to thunder crashing above.

"I'm here to tell the truth. I'm here to expose you for the liar that you are, Mr. Pious Almighty."

Carpious leans into Alethea with his finger mere inches from her face.

"Leave now or I *will* call the police again. And *this* time you won't get out! They will lock your scandalous—"

"Motherfucka, I will bleed you where you stand. You better step the fu—"

Carpious plunges his free hand uninvited into the right side of Alethea's face interrupting her words and repartee. The strength of his arm and the force of his closed fist knock Alethea off balance into dense, thorny shrubbery at the foot of the porch.

Carpious bends over and stabs his arm into the bushes after Alethea and yanks her out flinging her down on the wet ground in front of him. "I told you to never come here again," he barks leaning over Alethea who has turned to show a bloodied face absent of fear.

"Motherfucka, you crazy? You hit *me*? I thought you was a *Christian* man, motherfucka! Look at you. Hitting a woman! Now the world will see you for who you really is."

"Carpious?" a faint voice calls.

Carpious jerks in the direction of the beckoning and sees Sydney and Solomon standing behind his parked car as rain pours down on all of them. Behind her is a small audience of his neighbors, including Bernie.

"Sydney. She made me do it. I warned her to stay away. She knows better. She knows who I am."

"Who you are? Sydney asks.

"He's the man who saved me while he was in prison," a voice from behind Carpious says.

Carpious turns to see a smiling Ian helping Alethea to her feet. He's holding a bloody shiv in his other hand, much like the one used to kill Herc in prison.

"Prison? Wh-what?" Sydney responds surprised.

"Yeah. Prison. This motherfucka done spent more time in the pokey than you spent on your knees with ex-boyfriends and bosses," Alethea retorts.

Carpious grimaces but says, "No. I can explain." He walks toward Sydney who is gripping Solomon closer to her.

"Is it true, Carpious?" Sydney begs.

"No. I mean, yes…but i-it's not like that," he stutters with his arms outstretched in some form of surrender.

"Is it true, Pious?" Sydney repeats.

Carpious' head is filled with the sounds of Sydney's questions, crashing thunder, and rainfall.

"NOOO!" he shouts.

Carpious wakes up grasping at his sheets and air as sweat streams down his naked chest. As he sits up in his bed in the dark, he can hear his own heartbeat in his ears and feel it thumping from inside his breast as if it's trying to escape from him. And outside, it's raining.

~

For the past two and a half weeks, Carpious has been traveling as a representative of his employer, Ardent Investments, conducting audits for several clients. Sleeping in three different hotels during his four-city trek has left Carpious longing for the comfort of his own bed. Last night was his first night home but rather than sleep in sound peace, his slumber was riddled with nightmares that are likely to have been aggravated by thoughts of his ex-wife's reappearance and the introduction of Ian, reminders of his former life.

The chorus of rain outside his bedroom window greets him from a waking dream as he slides out of bed and saunters to the bathroom. He's dragging his feet, but his size fourteens thud on the hardwoods as proof of his sheer weight and clumsiness. He clumsily throws back the seat on the toilet and it crashes against the tank as Carpious releases a heavy stream of urine into the bowl as if he hasn't urinated in days. He sways sleepily back and forth in place until he's done and then he flushes. He turns the handle of the faucet to the sink until a trickle of water flows out while flicking on the switch to the overhead light. His massive hands, under the command of his drowsiness, accidentally hit the switch to the ventilation fan as well. The loud whir of the motor above startles him and he quickly flicks it off. He looks in the mirror at his tired eyes as he leans on the counter of the sink as the water runs.

Carpious plunges both hands under the running, cold water. He leans down over the sink and splashes his face several times before turning the handle to stop the flow of water once again. He looks up into the mirror again as he reaches to the side of the sink for a hand towel. He stares into his own eyes as if he's looking for something. Or someone.

~

Though it's still raining on and off hours later, Carpious has decided to trim the shrubbery alongside his house. Sheer boredom, Saturday tradition, or an attempt to distract his troubled mind from the questionable significance of bad dreams force Carpious outside. The physical activity and therapeutic rain serve Carpious well as be busies himself in silence. The rainfall has abated to a cool mist; the snipping of hedge clippers is the only noise that can be heard apart from an occasional car speeding down the wet road in the distance.

Carpious' gaunt figure, dressed in blue jeans and a white T-shirt, is made stark by a green lawn and foliage. He's bent over clipping leaves like a sculptor etching details into clay. At times he wildly snips full branches away from the dense shrubbery while other times, he leans in close to study the shrubbery's form before extracting a leaf or two. The intricate science of his concentrative silence is suddenly broken.

"Bernie," Carpious turns to greet his neighbor after he catches a glimpse of him walking toward his lawn from his peripheral view. "What are you doing out here in the elements?"

"I could ask you the same thing, young blood. In case you haven't noticed, it's raining."

"Oh? This?" Carpious stretches his hands out, looking up. "This isn't rain. This is a refreshing sprinkle."

Bernie chuckles as he steps onto the porch for shelter from the rain.

"I haven't seen you in a while, since the last time we talked. I was wondering how that talk with our neighbor went."

Carpious is quiet for a moment looking down at the ground before he recovers from some secret thought and looks at Bernie with a smile.

"I didn't really get a chance to talk to him like I wanted to. I introduced myself to him but I had to cut my visit short because he had company. Don't worry. I'll talk to him and feel him out in due time."

Carpious concludes his short tale with a smile and a pat on Bernie's shoulder, thinking that he has satisfied his neighbor's inquisition, but Bernie is not content and is all the more curious.

"He had company? Who? Was it a woman or man?"
"Well, I didn't…"

At that moment, Sydney's SUV pulls into Carpious' driveway, rescuing him from the challenge of avoiding Bernie's barrage of questions.

"Looks like we're not the only ones out in the rain, huh Carpious?"

"I guess not," Carpious answers looking both relieved and surprised at the arrival of Sydney.

Solomon explodes out of the car door and excitedly calls out, "Carpious!!"

He wraps himself around Carpious' legs, holding him in place for Sydney to approach in her less aggressive form of hello. She hugs him tightly, but before kissing him, she exclaims, "Oh! You're soaking wet."

She pulls back from the hug and kisses him respectfully, aware that Bernie is standing there. Solomon has stopped hugging Carpious legs.

"Hi, Bernie. How are you?" Sydney greets.

"Hi, Mr. Bernie," Solomon follows.

Bernie lights up with a huge smile at the acknowledgement. "Hello, folks. It's a rainy weekend, isn't it?"

"I know. It feels like it's been raining nonstop for days. Carpious has missed out on all of this."

"It was sunny in Utah, but I'll take the rain over traveling. I couldn't *wait* to get home to this."

Carpious hugs Sydney and Solomon with an elation that makes her blush.

"Utah?" Bernie asks surprised.

"Yeah, Bern. Utah. I was there for close to three weeks for work. I just got in last night."

"I figured you would still be in the bed. We just came by to fix you some lunch and say hello," Sydney says.

"Oh, well let me get out of your hair. I was just speaking to our friend here. I hadn't seen his face around here in a while but obviously I'm not the only one who missed him."

"Bernie, you don't have to rush off. Would you like to stay for some lunch?"

"Oh, thank you, Sydney but I just ate. Thank you. I won't break up the family reunion," Bernie chuckles. "I'll catch up with you later, Carpious."

Bernie shuffles back across the street, covering his head as if it will shield him from the mist.

"Talk to you later, Bernie," Carpious calls as Bernie smiles and waves back.

"Bye," Sydney and Solomon sing in chorus.

Sydney turns her attention to Carpious. "Let's get you inside and dry. You have to tell us *all* about your trip."

"*And* you have to play me in dominos. I think I can beat you now."

"Is that so, Solo?"

Carpious wraps his arms around Sydney and Solomon as they head inside. The rain continues.

~

361 Mechi Lane seldom sees visitors. As a matter of fact, in the five months that Ian Kaplan has occupied the residence, Carpious is the only visitor who hasn't been there in some official, utilitarian, or delivery capacity. Ian hasn't taken any interest in getting to know his neighbors either. He appears content to live in seclusion, surrounded by an extremely social neighborhood setting.

A melancholy guitar blares over the stereo as Ian reclines across his couch with a laptop in front of him and a half empty bottle of wine beside him. On the floor are several books including *A Brief History of Time* by

Stephen Hawking, *Native Son* by Richard Wright, *The Waste Land* by T.S. Eliot, and a ragged Bible with half the cover missing. He's dressed in boxers, a T-shirt, and socks as if he just woke up, even though it's 7 p.m. The décor of his home is akin to a modern furniture catalog with all of the trendy colors and dark woods placed about. Though his home is well lit, there is no natural light from outside, for Ian keeps his curtains to the outside world drawn.

A tone-deaf Ian sings along with the music, "No stunt man surprises or Houdini-like disguises for a death-defying escape. Avoid the tap on the shoulder from that one in the long blaaack ca—"

A loud knock on the door interrupts Ian's melancholy solo. He turns the music down a bit and gets up from the couch with no haste. Even though he knows who is likely knocking, he peeks through the curtains.

As he returns the curtains to their original position, he musters a nervous smile and says loudly, "Hold on a second."

Ian opens the door slightly to see Carpious standing there with an expressionless look on his face.

"Pious!" Ian greets with only his head showing from behind the door.

"Don't call me that," Carpious says in a low rumble. "May I come in for a moment?"

Ian hesitates and returns, "Um…I'm not really dressed but…"

Carpious sighs impatiently, "Can you put some clothes on then? We need to finish our talk."

"Um, sure. Come on in."

Ian opens the door fully and Carpious steps inside. As Ian closes and locks the door, Carpious looks around.

"You've finally gotten all of your stuff together here, I see. You feel at home yet?"

"Actually, I do. Please have a seat."

Ian leads Carpious to a chair adjacent to the couch that he was previously sitting on. Carpious appears leery but moves a pillow aside and sits down in the olive green-striped chair that is dwarfed by his large size.

"Don't you want to put on some pants?"

"Nah. I'm fine. Don't worry. I won't try to rape you or anything."

Ian laughs as he sits and seems rather comfortable with Carpious there, but Carpious bristles at the joke and shows a clear flash of annoyance as he frowns back at him.

"Ian, the neighbors are restless about you being here. I said that I would talk to them in your favor as long as you didn't tell anyone that you know me, but…I'm not so sure. I mean, the more they dig up on you, the more likely my name will come up."

"So this is about *you*? I thought we were cool. I thought you already *talked* to our neighbors. I'm walking around like I've got nothing to worry about now, and you haven't said *anything*?"

"It's not as easy as that. And this *is* about me too. I've worked hard to change who I was and I don't want to have to go back and answer for what is in the past."

Ian leans forward. "Like *I* have to? I carry my sin with me everywhere I go. I don't have the luxury of recreating a life and starting all over from scratch. All I can do is try to show that I'm a different man than what people think and hope that they'll eventually forgive me. You and I are just alike, Carpious. You were just lucky to have committed a crime that has an expiration date on judgment. I, on the other hand, have to—"

Carpious interrupts, "You and I are *nothing* alike, Ian. You are a godless pedophile. You took away a little girl's innocence. Me? I murdered a man in self-defense. Our only connection is that this was the same man who raped you continually in prison and he took a shot at me and I killed him. I *had* no choice."

"Are you serious? A godless pedophile? What do you know about *God*, Dear Pontiff of Piety? I am *not* a pedophile! I made a mistake in judgment and I paid the price. I paid a *high* price and I'm not trying to hide it. I'm not trying to hide who I am because I hate myself. You look at me with judgmental eyes, but you're looking in a mirror. You hate the name *Pious* because it's a reminder of who you really are and where we both came from. You have no right to judge me. You are *just* like me."

Carpious stands up shaking his head and looks down at Ian who is still seated. They stare at each other in a silent standoff until Carpious speaks.

"You are not welcome in this neighborhood, Ian. I can't help you. You're on your own."

"I have just as much right to be here as you. Actually, I have *more* of a right. At least the people here know who I am and where I came from. They don't even know you."

"They do know me. And they love me. And accept me."

"Really? I can't wait until the next HOA meeting. We'll have a nice little time trading stories about Carpious, I'm sure."

"You're not welcome here, Ian. I'm sorry. It's not my call."

Ian stands. "So what do you advise that I do? *Pack up my shit and leave town, Sheriff?*"

"I don't know what to tell you. Maybe if you put a FOR SALE sign in front of your house, it'll seem like you're repentant and everyone will change their opinion of you."

"Deception? That's your advice? We may be alike, but I'm not you. I will not live a lie."

"Well then you will leave. Don't force my hand, Ian."

"Force your hand? What are you going to do? Stab me 126 times? Plant child porn on my computer? Make up lies about me? Concoct one of your deceptions?"

Carpious scoffs as he walks toward the door.

"You've gotten your eviction notice. Do the right thing. I'm sure this house will sell for more than you paid for it since you've done a few aesthetic things to the outside with the landscaping and all."

Ian gets up and follows Carpious to the door. "Are you sure you want to go down this road with me, Carpious? I may be a registered sex offender worth nothing to you but I'm also a wealthy, resourceful man with a lot of time on his hands."

Carpious abruptly turns and grabs the neckline of Ian's T-shirt with both hands and rumbles through a clenched jaw, "Are you threatening me, you little shit?"

Ian is calm as he jerks out of Carpious' hold and steps back. He reaches to unlock the door and opens it.

"I wasn't threatening you. I was mirroring you. I don't wish to be enemies, but you've crossed the line, *Pious*! Now *this* is a threat: you come to my home again, I *will* shoot you as an intruder. Now *get* out!

Carpious steps onto the porch and the door slams behind him. Carpious feels the stares of several sets of eyes burning him as he walks away.

CHAPTER TWELVE

Carpious sits at his dining room table holding an envelope in one hand and a cell phone to his ear with the other. Spread about on the table are several pieces of opened mail and a laptop. Carpious is on hold with the party on the other end while he looks at the printed envelope in his hand intently; someone on the other end returns to the line.

"Yes? That's right. *Two* years. Yes. Would you please mail me a copy of that bill as well? Yes. Thank you. Yes, this is her husband. Would you confirm the mailing address that you have on record?"

Carpious puts the envelope down on the table and begins scribbling with a pencil what he's hearing. "Mmmhmm. Yes. That's correct. Thank you *so* much, ma'am. I'm so forgetful that it's best that I do this now. Mmm...I know. You have a great day too. Thank you."

Carpious hangs up the phone and looks at the envelope with an arrogant smirk. He pulls his laptop closer to him and begins typing. A few moments pass before he writes something else down and concludes by closing the laptop and stuffing the envelope in his back pocket. He gets up from the table and grabs a folder and the car keys on his way out the side door. The garage door squeals open over the sound of the car starting. Moments later, it's once again silent and Carpious is gone.

Tales of the Wild West boast of rangers, derelicts, and desperados. The desperados were often times the underdogs, who, through a series of events, hit rock bottom on the run. These bad boys with a moral code would somehow become the heroes of the concluded story and ride off on dark horses into the sunlit horizon. Desperados are fictional.

The desperate man is real life. He is usually not the hero of the story; and the only horizon that he travels toward at the end of his tale is six feet below ground. The desperate man is dangerous, akin to a wounded feral cat trapped in a corner. No one knows—not even he—what he will do next.

~

Driving on the highway in Admah City can be taxing. Like many progressive cities, the commuting population has exceeded the planning of civil engineers. Road expansion is necessary to keep up with the demands of the populace; while at the same time, construction work and road rage hinder efficiency and safety.

Carpious is not bothered by the traffic, the exhausting orange cones, or the torn-up road as he veers along the highway. Sunday traffic is more forgiving and his attention is elsewhere. Typical of his home and car environment, music accompanies his focused silence.

An acoustic song of somber note is playing on the radio as the artist sings, "…many people say good-bye before they say hello, step into the morning and disapp—"

Carpious abruptly clicks the music off. "Damn depressing," he mumbles to himself.

Carpious' confrontation with Ian has left him on edge and thoughtful of how he's going to manage this powder keg of a situation. Some of the things that Ian said to him are still resonating within his consciousness—like the accusation that he was living a lie.

Is he *really* living a lie? Or is he simply aspiring to remain in the present? Why look backward or trouble others with what once was?

Several years ago, Carpious found much favor with Pastor Russell Moser, who helped him find work after being released from prison. Once he proved himself reformed, competent, and trustworthy, Carpious' past was spoken of no more. The principal at Ardent Investments and Moser's close friend, Leonard Matthias, retired shortly thereafter, so other than Human Resources, no one knows that Carpious has a criminal record.

Perhaps in arrogance of overcoming that insurmountable obstacle, he feels entitled to hide it from everyone else. But it has been said that it takes at least two lies to prop up one.

Carpious continues to drive in silence as he exits the highway. He's entering a much more congested part of Admah City near downtown and away from the quiet suburbia where he lives.

Here, there are a lot of trendy shops and places to eat as well as office and apartment buildings. He's become quite familiar with this area since he's been dating Sydney who lives and works here.

A push of a button and the windows slide down to let a breeze in as he makes several turns through various streets toward his destination. He's far away in thought and his expression is of slight agitation as he pulls into a complex of condos.

A stoned archway reading *Enclave Walk* in bold calligraphic letters greets Carpious as he drives past a security gate and smiling guard. He continues up a winding hill past manicured trees and landscaping until he reaches his destination: Sydney's home. He pauses and exhales deeply.

He retrieves the folder from the passenger seat, steps out of his car, and ascends a flight of stairs to her condo. A knock on the door yields Sydney, who is beaming at his presence. She greets him with a passionate hug.

"Hey, sweetie. I'm *so* happy to see you!"

Carpious hugs her back less passionately and coolly returns, "Likewise, dear."

Sydney takes Carpious by the hand and leads him inside.

"Solomon is next door at my friend's so that you and I can have some time alone without distractions, although you appear to have brought your own."

"Huh? My own? Oh. I'm sorry. I'm just…I just want to…"

Sydney grips Carpious' hand tighter and turns to look him in the eyes.

"Sweetie, it's okay, whatever it is. Come on. Let's sit on the patio."

Sydney leads Carpious from the living room to a sliding glass door on the other side of the spacious kitchen and dining area. The door opens onto a patio that overlooks a large, landscaped courtyard lined with flowers and stone benches and a large koi pond that is punctuated by a wooden bridge that arches across it. Evidenced by the reclining, padded chairs and accompanying end tables, Sydney has converted this simple patio into her own personal and peaceful refuge.

"Sit here, sweetie," she guides Carpious by the arm as he sits.

On one of the end tables is a bowl of hummus with triangles of pita bread lining the sides. Next to the bowl are two glasses filled with some indistinguishable beverage. Carpious picks up a cup to take a sip to calm his nerves. After one sample sip, he throws his head back and gulps the rest down in one swallow until only the clatter of ice remains.

"What is this?" he asks as Sydney reclines in the chair beside him.

"I've been experimenting with juicing so this is a combination of carrots, cucumbers, apples, beets, strawberries, and lime juice. Oh, and pineapples. Do you like it?"

Carpious holds up his empty glass and smiles, "Indeed."

"Do you want more?"

"Maybe later, Syd. I want to...I don't know how to even start to tell you..." Carpious sits up and exhales deeply while fumbling through the folder he brought along with him.

"Baby, I've *never* had the opportunity to know anyone like you—let alone to be *loved* by someone like you. If I'd met you years ago, I can't imagine how much better a man I would be because of you."

"Sweetie, you are..."

"Baby, please. This is the hardest thing that I've had to do, but I want to come clean with you because I love you and my heart is troubled that I've kept something from you. When we first started dating, we spent so little time consistently together that I didn't think we... I couldn't dredge up something from my past for what may have been a passing infatuation."

Carpious' voice trembles and he pauses for a moment to turn away from Sydney who is looking at him with compassion and intent.

He resumes, "You know that I was married before. I met Alethea while I was..." Carpious reaches into the folder and pulls out a set of papers that are stapled together. He hands them to Sydney.

He tries to continue talking, but words won't accompany his opened mouth as Sydney looks through the papers. He studies her as she's studying the papers. A frown slowly appears on her face.

"Carpious, are these *release* papers? You were in prison?"

Carpious looks at Sydney with a wide-eyed, fearful expression before he says, "Yes."

Sydney exhales, "Carpious, I don't know what to say. How? Why didn't you...?"

"When I was a kid, I got into some trouble. I fought a lot. I was angry about my mom dying, leaving me alone, but there is no excuse. Once I was in the system for a petty crime, I got sucked in further when I...when I killed a man."

"No..."

"It was self defense. He was going to kill me. It was self defense, Sydney. While I was in, I got close to God and changed my head around. I started studying and focusing on getting better. I started helping others and then the system had mercy on me. Toward the end of my sentence, I started corresponding with Alethea. That's how we met. I never met her until I was released."

Carpious pauses and looks down again.

"I'm sorry that I've kept this from you, but I love you too much to continue to do so. Even if you can't forgive me, you deserve to know."

Sydney springs from her chair, and, kneeling before Carpious with one hand on his knee and the other on the side of his face, she looks at him and says, "Forgive you, Carpious? Sweetie, don't you realize that this makes you a greater man than the one I knew ten minutes ago?"

Carpious locks eyes with Sydney as tears stream down her face.

"I don't know who you *were*. I know who you *are*. You have an amazing story to tell, Carpious. The difference your struggle made. The difference *you* can make. What God has done through you. You are *the* most amazing man to trust me. Forgive you? I have nothing against you. I love you."

Carpious embraces Sydney in that moment tighter than he's held anyone before.

Suddenly, he feels like he could tell her everything. If she were this receptive to his being an ex-con, *maybe* she would hear his true confession. Maybe she could emancipate him forever from the shame that his father molested him repeatedly.

Carpious pulls from Sydney's embrace to look her in the eyes once more.

"This is it!" he subconsciously exclaims. "Freedom."

Freedom from the prison that he's created. Freedom from the secrets and the duplicity. Freedom to move forward.

Carpious opens his mouth to expel the remainder of his confession, but instead, all that he releases is a sigh.

~

A few hours have passed and it's close to midnight. Carpious told Sydney that he needed to get home to prepare for an early morning at work. They'd spent more time talking about his past, but he didn't yield more details about the real reason of his deceit. He distracted Sydney from asking particular questions about why he initially went to jail with tales of his religious conversion and of his completing a college degree in accounting. He even detailed the horrific account of Herc's murder, minus the part about stabbing him one hundred and twenty-six times. Self-defense is what *he* called it—not murder.

Usually after such an agonizing confession, one would likely be elated with a sense of newfound freedom from secrecy, but Carpious doesn't feel free. Where he isn't numb, he's anxious about another matter—a matter on which all of his intent and being is focused at the moment.

He doesn't drive long before he pulls his car over to a dark curbside near a row of upscale condos. He turns off the overhead lights inside before opening the door. Rather than slam the car door, he quietly uses his hips to close it. As he locks the car with his key instead of the remote, he checks his surroundings.

The immediate vicinity is quiet, but as Carpious walks in the shadows away from his parked car, he nears a busier area of public housing and people where darkness is the only indication that it's past midnight. Distant sirens get closer, mingling with the sounds of people conversing, laughing, cursing, and soliciting.

The charming smile that Carpious typically wears is absent now as he walks briskly with his hands stuffed in his jacket pockets. He nears a group of four younger men who are huddled in the middle of the sidewalk. The men see him approaching and one steps into Carpious' path and says, "What's yo pleasure, dog?"

Carpious stops in front of him and looks around before looking at the man again and asking, "What?"

"What you need, old man?"

"Whatever you got that's not baking soda or parsley from your mom's kitchen."

The man bristles at the mention of his mom, but Carpious doesn't flinch or look away.

"You wanna get amped? I got some o' that white girl. You wanna get low, I got some o' that Jane."

"Uh…amped. Two bags."

"That's a C."

Carpious frowns. "What?"

"A hundred, pops. Damn, son. Where you from?"

Carpious pulls one hand out of his pocket to reveal a black-gloved hand holding a roll of ten-dollar bills. He hands them to the man who counts them. The man turns to his friends and flashes two fingers and wipes under his nose as another of the men approaches and brandishes two small bags of cocaine. He hands them to Carpious who stuffs the bags in his pocket. The others start to move in closer.

Carpious sees their intent and glares at them saying, "You gentlemen best step back before I take my *other* hand out of my pocket. And it's *not* holding another roll of tens."

The men move aside as a tense-jawed Carpious continues past them in the direction he was walking.

~

Several minutes of walking later, Carpious slows to a string of weathered, duplex homes off of the busy street. It's quieter in this neighborhood and most of the houses appear dark inside. Carpious reaches into his back pocket to retrieve the envelope that he wrote on earlier. Using traces of dim light from a street lamp, he looks at the envelope and then at the clutch of mailboxes.

Carpious scrutinizes the area and pads across the lawn to one of the windows of the duplex. He examines the driveway to see that there is no car parked in front like the truck parked in the driveway of the connecting unit.

Despite his height, he has to stand on his toes to look into the kitchen window. Though it's mostly dark inside, he sees evidence of a dim, dancing light coming from down the hallway.

He stalks to the back door and reaches into his pocket for a long flat piece of metal similar to a screwdriver. He slides it in between the door and the doorframe near the lock and turns the doorknob with his other gloved hand. The door opens.

Carpious moves inside and pauses every two steps to listen. The light coming from down the hall is a television with the volume low, but it's likely that no one is watching it as it appears that no one is home. He makes his way to what appears to be an office or a den. He picks up a framed picture from a desk and looks at it from an angle to catch the light from the hallway.

"Alethea," he mutters to himself.

Carpious looks around the room and sees another picture on the wall of Alethea and two other women. The picture appears to be five to ten years old.

Carpious reaches into his pocket and takes out one of the bags of cocaine. He slides one of the drawers open and places the bag deep in the back of the drawer before sliding it closed again.

He tiptoes to the kitchen and opens the refrigerator. The light that comes on from inside when he opens the door startles him. He quickly places the other bag of cocaine in the back of the freezer out of plain sight.

Carpious quietly leaves out the way he came as if he were never there.

~

Thirty-five minutes later, Carpious returns to his parked car. He reaches in his back pocket for the envelope again, and, as he gets in and starts the engine, he dials a number that is scribbled on the envelope.

He waits several moments before answering, "Yes, is this the parole officer of an Alethea Mightson? Yes…I'm aware of the hour, sir, but this is a time-sensitive matter that may endanger my family. This is a neighbor of hers and I have a concern to discuss with you."

CHAPTER THIRTEEN

It's a beautiful day in the Mechi Lane neighborhood. The pigments of spring have become evident following a couple of weeks of non-stop April showers. Hues of green saturate the ground as well as the trees. Intense dyes of yellow, white, purple, and red are sprinkled on nature's canvas.

Shoots of grass take the place of predecessors that were mowed down just a week ago. The soil is a damp smorgasbord for the robins as they flit back and forth with nutritious treasures to present to their nestlings in the trees above. A male cardinal looks like a lone holly berry in a bush singing his repetitive mating song while several other species of birds serenade in the background.

The roar of several lawnmowers competes with the giggles and laughter of neighborhood children playing. Carpious is carrying out his Saturday ritual of yard maintenance and he is not alone. Bernie stuffs grass cuttings into a lawn bag that will soon join the other two already in front of his house on the curbside. Next door, Lela is sitting on the porch holding a restless Caleb and watching Haleigh play down the street with the other kids. Many neighbors busy themselves, attending to yard work, exercising, relaxing, and socializing with one another.

At the cul-de-sac, there is no sign of participation from Ian, as usual. Despite the gorgeous, sunny day, his curtains are drawn and his car is hidden from view so there is no indication as to whether he's home or not. His lawn has already been attended to by a professional lawn service. Ian's house is one of the newer ones on Mechi Lane and the lone dogwood sapling in front is an indication of its newness. The tree stands no taller than eight feet but the blizzard of white blossoms that complement the deep green leaves give the illusion that it's larger and denser than it really is.

Bernie stuffs the last bit of grass and sticks into a lawn bag as Carpious approaches. On his way across the street, he smiles and waves at a few neighbors like some politician desperately bent on winning an election.

"You've been busy here, Bern," Carpious greets.

Bernie, still bent over with his arm halfway in the lawn bag, turns awkwardly before straightening up and brushing his hands on his gray sweater.

"Hey there, Carpious!" Bernie smiles as he reaches for Carpious' hand to shake. "Yeah, I had a burst of energy this morning when the sun came out. I see that I wasn't the only one though." Bernie waves his hand in the direction of the rest of the neighborhood.

"Yes, Mechi Lane is abuzz with activity. It's a beautiful day." Carpious looks at Bernie and there is a moment of uncomfortable silence on his part before he continues, "You know, I finally talked to our new neighbor."

"This body is tired of standing. Come on, let's sit for a few."

Bernie shuffles to his porch and falls into a seated position. Carpious remains standing with one foot propped on a step.

"I talked to him the other day but, it didn't go too well."

Carpious shakes his head with a frown before turning to Bernie with an intense look on his face. "I went over to talk to him, like you asked. I introduced myself and told him about our community and how family was important to us. I never accused him of anything but he immediately got suspicious of my intentions and told me to leave his home. I tried to reason with him and told him about how some of the parents here are nervous about his presence. I suggested that he try—try—to get out and meet the neighbors, let them see his face and hear his voice. He just became more defensive, like he had something to hide."

Bernie looks down the street shaking his head. "Times sure have changed. There was once a time where people like that wouldn't be allowed in town, let alone in a neighborhood where innocent children play."

"Yeah. Anyone who would do that to children..."

"Not just them. Ex-cons, period. I don't believe for a second that any of them change. I've read the statistics of how most of them learn how to be better criminals in prison. So they get out and they're more dangerous."

"Well I...I think we just need to watch him. Watch his every move. We're a family here. If he doesn't want to be a part of it, he doesn't belong here. But, hey, look, I'm not trying to dampen this beautiful day."

Bernie nods thoughtfully. "You're right. We should invite him to dinner."

Carpious' eyes widen and he straightens up, as he looks dumbfounded at Bernie. "What?"

"We should invite him to dinner; reach out to him; make him feel comfortable. How does the saying go? 'Keep your friends close and your enemies closer'? Don't you think it's a good idea?"

"I-I don't know, Bern. Quoting Sun Tzu sounds ideal but what if his response isn't favorable? What if he just responds to the invitation the way he responded to me? What if he thinks we're just trying to set him up for something? Maybe we should leave well enough alone and just watch him. Maybe he'll come around in his own time."

"Nah, I think I'm on to something," Bernie protests as he holds his finger in front of his lips with a puzzling look. "*Times* have changed, but that doesn't mean that *we* have to. There was once a kinder, gentler time when you would take an apple pie to the new neighbor and have a conversation with him and see what he was all about. There was a sense of community when all of your neighbors knew about each other, and if they had a problem, they didn't go all secretive and draw the curtains and isolate themselves."

"So, what are you going to do? Just walk right up to his door and invite him to your house?"

"Yes. How would you do it? How else can I see what he's about except by looking him dead in the eyes?" Bernie laughs heartily.

Carpious looks away troubled, but Bernie is silent and smiling, satisfied with his resolution.

~

Across the street, young Caleb joins the chorus of spring. Though he hasn't slept quietly in close to twenty-four hours, his lungs don't seem to show any evidence of fatigue. Lela thought that by sitting on the porch with him amidst all of the activity and sounds of the day, that he might settle down and perhaps take a nap. No such fortune.

She bounces him on her shoulder as they rock back and forth in the swing.

"Shhhhh. Someone is soooo sleepy. Someone is fighting it sooooo much. Come on, Caleb baby...shhhhhhh."

The door swings open onto the porch and Drew peers out.

"Lela, why is he still crying? I'm trying to review these functional requirements, but I can't concentrate. Isn't there something you can give him?"

"Drew, he's probably crying because he's gassy. There's nothing I can do about that but try to get him to pass those air bubbles. What do you suggest—that I drug him? If you don't want to be here..."

"I'm not saying I don't want to be here. I'm just concerned that Cale—"

"Don't try to make this about Caleb, Drew. You're thinking about yourself once again. You haven't so much as offered to help me. Caleb responds to you; perhaps if you helped to get him settled, he would go to sleep and you could finish your work."

"I stayed home because you say that I don't spend enough time here. The reason why I usually stay in the office is because I can't concentrate. What do you want from me? It's like I can't win."

Lela sighs and looks away from Drew as she continues to try to soothe Caleb. Drew lingers in the door for a moment and opens his mouth to say something when his phone vibrates in his pocket. He goes back inside.

Haleigh runs from across the street with several other little kids in tow.

"Mommy," Haleigh inquires halfway out of breath.

"Yes, dear."

"Why is Caleb crying?"

"His tummy hurts and he's sleepy."

"Where's Daddy?"

"He's inside working."

"Oh. Can I go play in Nadia's backyard? We were going to play kick ball."

"Honey, I don't think so. Where is her mom?

"Oh." Haleigh runs back across the street to the front porch of Nadia's house and says something to the screen door that Lela can't quite make out from the distance. Then the screen door opens and Amril Flores, Nadia's mom, waves to Lela.

"It's okay. She's fine," Amril announces loudly.

Lela smiles and waves back without saying anything. Nadia opens the gate on the side of her house and lets Haleigh and the other children run into the backyard.

Amril Flores has been living at 230 Mechi Lane for a little over seven years now. When she and her husband moved there from Guyana, she was pregnant with Nadia who is now Haleigh's age. Lela and Amril are relatively close because their daughters are in the same class at school and play together a lot.

As Lela continues to rub Caleb's back and lull him to sleep, the garage door whines open as Drew backs out. He lets down the window to the passenger side and leans over to address Lela.

"I'm going to run to the office. I'll be back before eight."

Lela doesn't acknowledge Drew with an answer, or so much as a nod, nor does he wait for one. He continues out of the driveway, and as he leaves, waves to Carpious, who is walking back across the street to his house.

~

Carpious walks up his driveway after spending a few more moments with Bernie talking about things that didn't involve Ian or uncomfortable silences. He was unsure of how to distract Bernie from inviting their mysterious neighbor to dinner. The last exchange that he'd had with Ian gave Carpious every indication that Ian might try to expose his past in the worst way.

Lela calls to Carpious from her swing on the porch, "Carpious, are you going inside now?"

Carpious' attention is redirected. "Lela, hey. What do you need?" he answers as he walks over toward her.

"I think I'm going to put Caleb down and take a nap while he's out. I'm *so* exhausted. I told Haleigh she could play at Amril's for a little bit. She's in the backyard. Would you keep an eye on her for me? I'll come by to get her after my nap."

"Of course, I'll watch her. You get some rest. No worries."

"Thank you so much, Carpious. You're an angel."

Carpious smiles while thinking of the label that has been bestowed on him: angel.

Would Lela think her charming neighbor was of such angelic nature if she knew that he served sixteen years in prison for felonious murder and before that, tried to murder his stepfather who molested him? Would she trust him with her daughter if she knew that he and the new neighbor, who was a registered sex offender, had some degree of a connection?

Lela gently gets up from the swing so as to not wake Caleb.

Carpious trots up the steps to open the door for Lela and he quietly closes it behind her as she mouths, "Thank you."

~

Nadia Flores is running as hard as she's ever run in her short life. Though her eyes are closed tightly, she knows where her gazelle-like bounds will take her. Screams all around her are taunting and cheering all at once. Her feet pound the soil as her heart pounds inside her chest. She opens her eyes for a split second to see a red blur coming at her. Instinct and fear jerk her downward as she dodges the red blur that flies past her. She leaps into the air and lands on home plate. All of the other kids on her team cheer and chant Nadia's name as this was the tiebreaker in the Mechi Lane Kickball Championship Game of the World—at least that's what they named it.

A dozen children varying from the ages of six to twelve are playing in Amril Flores' backyard. For some reason, this has always been the congregation area for the neighborhood children to play. Perhaps it's due to the immense size of the backyard, complemented by a swing set in the far corner, and complete with a slide and monkey bars. Perhaps some prefer it because of the high fence and its tolerance for high-flying balls. Or perhaps some are simple enough in their tastes to prefer it because Amril Flores always has some kind of treat for all in attendance. Today, it was popsicles during halftime. Cherry, orange, and grape stains join the dirt and grass smears across the kids' clothing now. Haleigh's sleeve is barely hanging onto her T-shirt from an earlier struggle at third base. Ten-year-old Ethan obviously confused the rules of kickball with the standards of football as he tackled Haleigh to keep her from accomplishing much more than third base as she'd kicked a home run.

The children have been playing and screaming for about an hour now, but they aren't ready to retire to their homes and bath time just yet.

"Who wants to play hide-and-seek?" Gabe challenges.

"Ooooh, I do," shouts Kenya.

"Me too," echoe Alex and Cristina.

"Vic, is it," Alex yells. "No, I'm not!" cries Vic.

"Kiara, can be it. She runs the fastest," Tristan volunteers.

Kiara agrees as Haleigh, Eli, Quan, and Nadia register their votes in affirmation.

"There's nowhere to hide back here," Cristina announces, speaking of the Flores' backyard.

"Let's play out in front."

"Yeah, we have more hiding places."

"This is going to be awesome!"

The children run to the front yard in unison.

"Home base is the front porch," Kenya declares. "I'm counting to twenty."

Eleven-year-old Kenya begins counting loudly with her back turned to the street and her eyes closed as she leans on the porch banister. Mechi Lane is such a haven for the children there that they see no reason to confine their hiding to the Flores' front yard, so they scatter into the streets, behind the cars, trees, and bushes of the other neighbors.

Haleigh, determined to find the perfect hiding place, runs the furthest and tucks behind the trashcan in front of 361 Mechi Lane—Ian's house.

From afar she can hear the count concluding, "Sixteen, seventeen, eighteen…"

Haleigh giggles to herself.

Suddenly, the door bursts open to Ian's house.

"Hey! What are you doing there, little girl? You can't play here!"

Haleigh is so startled that she physically jumps up and bumps into the metal can that she was crouched behind. The top falls off and crashes to the ground as Haleigh nicks her chest on the metal's edge. Soggy, putrid trash falls out and to the ground.

"Eeeeeeeeeeeeeeee!" she screams, both from fear and pain and runs away.

Ian looks around hoping that there were witnesses to his protest. Children make him nervous, and justly so, since he went to prison for his inappropriate association with one.

Haleigh runs past the Flores' house toward home screaming and crying and holding her arm to her chest that is bleeding from the deep scratch of the trash can edge.

Carpious, who is sitting on the porch reading, leaps up at hearing Haleigh's cries. He runs out to meet her and kneels to pick her up.

"Eeeeeeeeeeaughhhh!" Haleigh screams.

"Haleigh, baby, what happened?"

Haleigh is crying and squealing and speaking incoherently.

Carpious is holding her tightly and looking around for any evidence of what happened to her. He looks up the street and sees the gathering of children. A few are walking toward him.

"Haleigh, what's wrong? Are you hurt?"

Carpious lifts Hailey up to inspect her and sees the blood on her shirt and the torn sleeve. She's still crying and clawing for him to hold her close again.

"Come on. Let's get you inside and get you patched up."

Carpious holds a crying Haleigh over his shoulder and swings his front door open to take her inside. He dashes to the bathroom still holding her and grabs peroxide, bandages, and aspirin.

~

Carpious returns a bandaged and sleeping Haleigh to her mom next door forty-five minutes later.

"What happened?" Lela exclaims, seeing a bandage peeking out of the neckline of a new T-shirt.

"As far as I can tell, she got hurt playing with the kids," Carpious answers. "She was screaming so much I couldn't get anything out of her. By the time she calmed down, she'd cried herself to sleep. I'll go check with Amril to see what happened. Don't you worry."

"Thank you *so* much, Carpious. Once again, you're our hero."

"No problem, Lela."

Carpious leaves the Jansons' and walks across the street as one of the children from earlier stops him.

"Is Haleigh okay?" Kenya asks.

"Yes, she's sleeping. She'll be fine."

Carpious kneels on the sidewalk in front of Kenya to get on her eye level. "What happened? How did she get hurt?"

"We were playing hide-and-seek and then she just started screaming and running away. I think that man did something to her."

"What man?" Carpious fires back in a piercing tone.

Kenya points up the street toward Ian's house. "The man that my momma said is a bad man 'cause he hurt children. *That* man."

Carpious squints and his jaws tighten.

CHAPTER FOURTEEN

Darkness has fallen over Mechi Lane and the sound of spring and children laughing and neighbors milling about have subsided, allowing the songs of crickets and cicadas to be heard. The occupants of the houses of Mechi Lane have retreated to eat, sleep, or prepare for the next day. Most of the occupants have retreated to their abodes, except for Carpious.

Less than two hours ago, Carpious came to the conclusion that Ian had done something to hurt Haleigh. Unsure of the details, all he knows is that he has reason enough to confront him and use this opportunity to run him out of the neighborhood for once and for all.

Carpious is dressed in dark sweats and a black T-shirt as typical of when he goes running. He briskly walks in the direction of Ian's house. A car is backing out of 229. A dog barks as he passes 263. He says good evening to Floyd Riviera as he walks past 329. In moments, he's at 361 Mechi Lane.

He sternly walks up the driveway to the front porch. He stands there in silence for a moment before knocking vigorously. He stops and listens for any activity inside. No one answers but he can hear a television inside with the volume up high.

Carpious tries to look through the curtains to see if he can catch a glimpse of Ian, but he sees only that there are lights on inside. He looks around before leaving the porch and darting to the side of the house into the shadows. He's careful to not make a sound as he stalks around to the back door where the kitchen is located. He looks through the glass-paneled door and curtains that don't fully obscure his view, to see Ian reclined on the couch watching television.

Carpious reaches in his pocket for the tool that he used in a previous break-in. He crouches to his knee to slip the lock but he sees that there are three locks to the door. It's likely that at least one of those locks is a deadbolt, so he decides that there's no way that he can efficiently get in this way.

He puts the tool back in his pocket and takes out a pair of gloves. He puts on one glove and wraps the other around his gloved fist. As his eyes are trained on Ian, he breaks the glass of the bottom left panel of the door. Ian doesn't seem to hear it over the television.

Carpious releases all of the locks with his gloved hand. He swings the door open and tiptoes gingerly across the broken glass before closing and locking the door behind him. He takes a deep breath while wiping his brow of a bead of sweat before walking toward Ian who is still reclined and unaware of Carpious' presence. The light is on in the kitchen and bathroom and a dim lamp sits in the corner of the living room where Ian is.

Ian is watching cartoons and is amused by what he sees, as evidenced by a low, constant chuckle.

"Cartoons. How appropriate," Carpious' voice booms over the volume.

Ian is startled and swings around to see Carpious in eerie silhouette. "What the fuck?"

He immediately scrambles to his feet and while doing so, reaches to the floor just under the couch. As Ian stands up to face Carpious, he points a gun—a Glock 27, 40-caliber handgun with a custom nickel-plated handle. Though the legality of him having a gun is questionable, he's been nervous for the past couple of weeks that Carpious would instigate some trouble for him since their last conversation.

Carpious is calm while Ian stutters, "How did you get in?" Ian stretches his neck to look behind Carpious and sees the broken glass. His eyes widen and he appears concerned. "Are you serious? You *broke* into my *house*? I can shoot you now and no one would question me. You're an intruder and the evidence is right there."

"You *could* shoot me, but you won't. You'd go right back where you came from for even having that in your possession as a convicted felon. You *know* why I'm here. I know what you did."

Ian frowns in sheer confusion. "W-what? What are you talking about?"

"You don't belong here. This is a neighborhood full of little kids. What were you thinking?"

Carpious walks slowly toward Ian. He has his hands up but not in surrender. Ian straightens his arm and points the gun with more emphasis.

"I-I didn't do anything wrong. She was trespassing. Like *you* are."

"So what? You want to rip *my* blouse too, you sick freak?"

"W-what?"

"*What* is the question I should be asking you. What did you do to Haleigh?"

Ian looks confused again and slightly relaxes his aim of the gun. "I didn't do anything. I-I-I screamed at her to get out of my yard. I know what people would think. Kids make me nervous. I didn't do anything to her!"

"Like you didn't do anything to that thirteen-year-old girl?"

"What? You're a fine one to bring up the past here. You forget that you have one too?

"Sure, I have a past, but it doesn't involve me stripping the innocence from a *child* because I can't get my dick to respond to a real woman."

"You don't *know* me! People *can* change!"

"People like you *never* change. You just go into hiding and fool people into thinking that you're safe until your next unsuspecting victim comes along."

Ian relaxes his tone and demeanor and smiles. "Feel like you're talking to a mirror, don't you?"

"You're a piece of shit pedophile and you don't belong here!"

"I don't belong here? I belong here as much as you. We've already had this discussion once. And you forget...*I'm* holding the gun. Who are you to judge me? Speaking of such, *Pious*, I did a little bit of research on you. You may have some influential friends, but you also have some loved ones who are sworn enemies."

Carpious stops his slow advance on Ian and lowers his hands with a quizzical stare. "Who?"

"That's right—your ex-wife. She hates your guts, by the way, and it seems that you've amped enough bad blood with her that she's willing to tell everything just to see you suffer. I discovered that she's got a fondness for HIV medication like a common junkie. It's amazing the things that she was willing to say about you to score another hit. She also told me about your girlfriend. I've seen her around. She's got a sweet ass. Maybe I'll give her a call too."

Carpious lunges at Ian who is slow to react. Two hundred twenty pounds of momentum and rage sends Ian backward into a curio cabinet. Glass shatters as he drops the gun and falls to his side as ceramics and wood rain over him.

Carpious corrects his balance and throws a forearm in front of his face just as a large figurine is hurled at him. He blocks it and it shatters on the floor. Carpious hurls a size fourteen into Ian's ribs, lifting him off of the ground. Ian snarls as he recovers enough to block Carpious' follow-up kick by grabbing his foot and pushing back with enough force to throw him off balance. Carpious falls on his butt as Ian scrambles across the broken glass to retrieve his weapon that has slid into the kitchen. Glass cuts into his forearms and hands as he frantically drags his body across the floor. Carpious recovers his feet just as Ian grips the muzzle of the gun. He reaches down to grab his arm and yanks Ian to his feet while he's still holding onto the gun.

Carpious lands a fist across Ian's face; and then another punch so hard that Ian's veneers are thrown from his mouth and across the room. He looks at Ian's toothless guise with wide-eyed wonder.

"What the …?" But Carpious quickly recovers from his shock as Ian regains enough composure to raise the weapon in his direction.

Seizing Ian by both wrists, Carpious slams his hand against a wall until Ian drops the gun. Ian juts a knee into Carpious' groin and dives for the gun.

Carpious grabs a hold of Ian's shirt and jerks him upward, almost to his feet, away from the fallen weapon. Ian pivots to loosen himself, but loses his balance. He falls against the kitchen counter and slides across it, failing to regain his balance. As he falls, he takes several items from the counter with him. His rapid descent to the floor is interrupted by the edge of the connecting counter and a crack to the base of his head. He falls limp to the floor. Carpious is standing over him holding a torn shirt that is still attached to Ian who is lying face down and still.

Carpious stands over Ian, sweating and breathing heavily, with the look of fear at what he's caused.

Ian lies sprawled among scattered kitchen utensils, motionless and silent.

Carpious' heavy, shallow breathing slows and deepens.

He stares at Ian.

Lying there.

So still. Unconscious. Lifeless. Dead?

And without warning,

Ian moves.

He flips himself over to his back and flails, trying to get up to no avail.

An abrupt and gargled cough sprays blood from his mouth and what sounds like, "H-help!" escapes his wet, red lips.

Ian thrashes his arms about, gasping as if he's drowning. He inhales deeply and a wet rattle inside his throat sputters and sprays his words. "C-call 911…my asth-ma…I can't…" Ian gasps.

Carpious drops the torn shirt and says nothing.

"I can't…move my…legs. My legs w-won't move… my chest is burning…p-please."

Carpious' face dims as he kneels over Ian.

"Help you? Help you to do what? Send me back to jail?"

"N-no…I won't…"

Ian breathes rapidly as he squirms on the floor drag-ging broken glass and utensils with him.

"No, Ian. I can't help you. Why would I?"

Ian exhales, "You…you …"

"I got my life together. I have a woman who accepts me for me even though she knows about my past. My co-workers and my community respect me. I'm *not* about to give that up for some Richie Rich pedophile who thinks he can buy his way out of every situation. I came here to force you to leave—not to *hurt* you. But you pointed a gun at me and now you want me to *help* you?"

Carpious stops and ponders. "No. I can't do it. I won't help you."

Carpious gets up and starts to back away from Ian who begins coughing and wheezing again as the over-spray of blood stains one side of his face.

"…but then you're a loose end. Not that anyone would care to visit you, but you might *not* die before someone did happen across you. Yeah, I can't let that happen. I've come too far. If you go away, that's it. One last loose end clipped and I'm free. Who's going to miss a pedophile?"

Carpious' eyes spark with violence as he slowly kneels over Ian once more. He begins talking in a gentle and calm voice. "Did you ever find out what happened to that girl you molested? Did she go on to live a normal life? Or did she eventually end her own life because she couldn't get the stench of your body out of her head? Do you ever think of what trouble you caused when you stuck your dick into a *child*?"

Ian fumbles with both hands across the floor and grabs a metal object and the wooden handle of a utensil. He swings the makeshift weapons wildly at Carpious who puts an arm up to block them but fails to protect himself from both.

A long barbecue fork stabs deeply into Carpious' arm. He backhands Ian with a closed fist and stumbles to his feet as he removes the fork from his left bicep. He kicks all of the remaining objects near Ian's grasp away as he surveys fallen items on the floor. He reaches for a dishtowel just beyond Ian's head. It's mostly white with green shades of plaid. He lays it over Ian's face.

Carpious lowers himself over Ian once again and rests one of his knees on Ian's chest as he relaxes his weight. Ian immediately begins to struggle to breathe as his arms flail uselessly in Carpious' direction.

Ian gasps and is unable to talk but as he wrenches his head from side to side, the dishtowel falls off of his face. He locks eyes with Carpious and begs in silence for mercy as Carpious glares back unfeeling.

Carpious returns the towel to his face and holds it in place with his fingers as both of his thumbs press into Ian's throat, constricting his airway even further. Ian bucks violently but paralysis is beginning to affect the accuracy of what little movement he has left.

A stray, clawing swing glances Carpious across the face, drawing blood from over his right brow. Blood stings his eye as it trails down his face, but he refuses to release his grip.

Carpious leans onto Ian's chest harder and squeezes his thumbs together tighter as his own arm oozes red. Blood spills down his arm to his stubborn and anchored fingers.

Ian begins to flail like a fish gasping desperately for air.

Carpious says nothing and Ian slowly stops struggling, as the towel over his face bleeds red both from Carpious' wound and from Ian's mouth.

And then the muffled moaning, blood spitting, and body thumping cease.

There is silence.

Under the weight and hands of his once-savior, Ian is dead.

"The weak can never forgive. Forgiveness is the attribute of the strong."

—*Mahatma Gandhi*

CHAPTER FIFTEEN

Smoke dances near Carpious' eyes, carrying dust and burning fragments too weightless to remain anchored in the fire that spawned them. He towers over the smoldering embers, sifting the ashes with a broad stick resembling the handle of a garden tool. It's the dawn of a new day—a Sunday —a day of worship for many, but rather than worship the God that he professes to yield his sins to, Carpious sees it more imperative to hide his sins.

Less than seven hours ago, Carpious extinguished the life of Ian Kaplan with extreme prejudice and brutality. Carpious' intent, when he broke into Ian's home, was not to kill him but to intimidate him to the point of leaving Mechi Lane and taking Carpious' secret with him. Things did not work out as he intended.

Now, a man lies dead on his kitchen floor as the murderer stands in his own backyard, burning the clothes he was wearing during the heinous act. Smoldering leaves and sticks camouflage the clothes that are now mere ashes, yet the memory and the guilt that accompany the deed are impervious to flame or any physical attempt at destruction. Carpious has taken several showers, but his thoughts are still bloodied by the memory of watching the life drain from Ian as he struggled for air. Carpious' arm is wrapped tightly in gauze and throbs with pain. A nagging remorse has taken residence in his heart as he ponders what he will do to distance himself from association and any suspicion once Ian's body is discovered.

Columns of thick, black smoke ascend into the blue sky, contrasting with the signs of spring and the crisp morning air. The acrid stench of burning wood is more suiting for a cold, windy fall day than the first morning of May. Carpious is grim and emotionless as he rakes more leaves and twigs into the altar of flames.

"Carpious?" a small voice calls from behind him. He's visibly startled as he jumps and turns to see who's there.

"Lela, good morning" Carpious feigns a smile. "I was deep in thought there. How are you this morning?"

Lela is holding Caleb as she stands at a safe distance from the fire. "I'm good, Carpious. Thanks. I thought your house was on fire or something. What's going on?"

"Is the smoke bothering you? I'm sorry."

"No. No. I just came outside to sit on the porch when I smelled smoke. My first thought was that something was burning over here."

"Yeah. I cut down a lot of trees back here yesterday and, uh, thought that it would be easier to burn the cuttings rather than chop them. I'm pretty certain that the trash people won't pick up some of the larger pieces."

"I see. What happened to your…?" Lela points at the small bandage across Carpious' right brow. Carpious reaches to touch his face.

"What? Oh, one of those branches caught me earlier. I'm not too handy with the ax after all. Fortunately, I turned my head right when the splintered piece flew at my face or I'd be wearing an eye patch instead of a bandage."

Lela bounces a smiling Caleb, watching as Carpious resumes aggravating the flames in silence. He nudges the last of the sticks into the fire before turning his attention to Lela.

"How is Haleigh doing?" he asks.

"Oh, she's still sleeping. I gave her some more aspirin for the scratch on her chest. She had a rough day yesterday, huh?"

"Yeah. It seems like it. I was worried about her. Did she tell you what happened? I couldn't get anything out of her because she was so upset."

"Oh, yes. That ugly scratch on her chest came from bumping into one of the neighbors' trashcans when the kids were playing hide-and-seek."

"Yeah, it was a pretty ugly cut, but I cleaned and disinfected it. I've learned a couple of tricks from Sydney, you know. How is it looking?"

"The swelling went down so she should be fine. She was hiding in that new guy's yard. What's his name?"

Carpious frowns, feigning ignorance. "Kipling? Kaplan? Ian Kaplan, I think."

"Yeah, that's it—the sex offender guy. She was hiding from the other kids in front of his house behind the trashcans and he came outside and yelled at her to get out of his yard."

"He yelled at her?" Carpious instigates. "What else happened? Did he touch her?"

"Heavens no! He simply startled her and that coupled with the scratch was why she was so upset."

"But, her clothes were torn and all the blood…I thought…"

"You know Haleigh. She plays like she's a little boy. You should see all of the torn dresses she went through before I started dressing her more like the tomboy she is."

Carpious' eyes widen as he struggles to comprehend Ian's implied innocence.

"So…he didn't do anything to her? He just *yelled* at her? He didn't touch her or *anything*?"

"Carpious, why would you think that? I know he went to jail for messing with a girl long time ago, but I don't think they would let him move into a neighborhood full of kids if he wasn't safe. Heaven forbid what her father would do to him if he did something to Haleigh, Drew may not win husband-of-the-year, but I can imagine he would do anything for the well-being of his daughter."

Carpious is silent as he looks at the ground, perplexed and shocked.

"Are you okay, Carpious? You look as pale as me."

Carpious looks up and tries to laugh at Lela's joke but only a smile comes forth. "So…where is Drew?" he redirects the conversation.

"I don't know. He didn't come home until late last night and he was gone this morning when I got up." Lela pauses while visibly trying to compose herself. "I don't mean to dump all of this on you, Carpious. Forgive me. I'm letting my feelings get the best of me. I'm sorry."

"No no, It's okay. Sometimes we let our emotions take over, do things that we wouldn't normally do in our right mind. That's what makes us human, right?"

Lela chuckles. "I guess. God knows *I'm* human."

Lela laughs as Carpious looks back to regard the smoldering fire. He frowns thoughtfully and turns back to Lela. "So, you don't think Drew would do anything crazy?"

"What do you mean?"

"If Ian had hurt Haleigh, you don't think he would do anything crazy, do you?"

"The Drew I know has a level head, so no, he wouldn't. But to be honest, I'm beginning to lose hope in what I think I know about Drew."

Carpious simply nods his head. His rage had deceived him into a rationalization that his act of homicide was justified—that Ian deserved his demise.

But now, the discovery that Ian was *not* guilty reveals to Carpious that last night, he acted as no less than judge and executioner.

~

Sunday draws to an early conclusion for Solomon Durden as his mother kisses him goodnight.

"Mommy, do I have to go to school tomorrow?" Solomon asks as he nestles between the sheets and his pillow.

"Of course, honey," Sydney answers.

"Can't I just stay home with you?"

"Spring break is over, honey bun. You have to go to school and I have to go to work tomorrow. Our vacation is over."

"Aw man."

"Aw man. I know," Sydney teases.

"Stop copying me."

"*You* stop copying me."

Solomon giggles as she leans in to kiss him.

"Night night, love."

"Night night, Mom."

Sydney flips the light switch off, leaving a dim night-light to glow near Solomon's bed. She pulls the door halfway closed and exhales a sigh of relief. It's been a long week, keeping an eight-year-old entertained.

This evening marks the end of impromptu field trips, long days in the park, the preparation of three meals, and consecutive late movie nights. This moment marks a return to normalcy.

Sydney has scant energy right now but an active son hasn't sapped it. No. Her energy has been sapped by words.

She's been playing back the words Carpious spoke to her the other day. Her initial response to those words felt right—the right thing to say. The passage of time has challenged those feelings and Sydney is considering how she *really* feels apart from how she is *supposed* to feel. As irony would have it, the words of Pastor Russell Moser defy her previous stance as well. The words he spoke today during his sermon in church echo in her head even now.

"Most people understand the necessity of forgiveness as beginning with the same circumstance one has caused another to suffer. Suffering creates a chasm between the opposing sides and makes it difficult to return to the point of solidarity where they once were. Whether the relationship was family, friendship, romantic, or business, there is pain and a sense of betrayal that has taken the place of what was once good.

"Some people think that the act of forgiveness is simply to deny that pain and sense of betrayal. They lie to themselves and try to move past the point of conflict only to develop more bitterness. This is not forgiveness at all. True forgiveness is not manufactured in the feeling that one has done the *right thing*. True forgiveness can hurt, sometimes more than the betrayal, but *that* pain is temporary, for true forgiveness is a means to healing."

Sydney offered Carpious words of unsolicited encouragement when she said she had nothing against him. While he was afraid that she was going to pull away from him in the face of the fact that he'd served time in prison for murder, she drew closer—at least superficially. Now her actions would need to follow suit or else she would appear to be insincere—and she was all too familiar with insincerity and it was not something she tolerated, especially in herself.

Her ex-husband, and Solomon's father, was insincere when he professed to love her and be faithful to her. One day, Sydney accidentally discovered his infidelity and, as a result, learned that all five years of their marriage were built on a lie. This man, who *she* truly did love and was faithful to, was living a secret life with another family. The true insincerity of it all was that he wouldn't even confess to it. There was a woman, a child, a house, and a bank account tied to another woman and her ex-husband wouldn't confess.

Sydney doesn't want to be that liar, so she allows all of her feelings to surface so that she may deal with them. Carpious trusted her with *his* truth, so she owes him the same transparency.

Sydney walks into the kitchen and begins the usual, end-of-the-day ritual of cleaning. As she cycles from the dishwasher to the cabinet, she notices a blinking red light on the answering machine at the end of the counter. She'd been so busy with cooking dinner and entertaining Solomon that she didn't notice that she had four messages. She pushes the play button to listen.

"BEEP. Sunday, 12:45 a.m."

"Hey. I can't sleep a-and I thought maybe there was a chance that you were still awake. I guess I was so tired that I fell asleep earlier than usual a few hours ago. A bad dream woke me up just now and, well, I just wanted to hear your voice."

There is a long pause.

"Well…you're sleeping, so hopefully I'll drift off again shortly. I'll see you in the morning at church. I love you. Night."

"BEEP. Sunday, 6:13 a.m."

"Good morning, baby. I'm not feeling all that well. I feel…feverish. Maybe its allergies or something, but I'm going to stay home this morning. I know you and Solomon have a lot of things planned for the day, so I guess I'll talk to you later on this evening. Don't worry about me. I just need to rest. Love you."

"BEEP. Sunday, 10:09 a.m."

" …this is the Admah City Symphony Orchestra and we value your donations…"

"BEEP. Sunday, 7:31 p.m."

"Sydney, give me a call when you get in and get settled, okay? I want to hear your voice, hear how your day went with Solomon and his friends and church and all. Love you."

Sydney frowns, confused as she listens to the last message left by Carpious. She picks up and inspects the phone connected to the answering machine and sees the cordless receiver's ringer has been switched to MUTE.

"Solomon," she resolves as she recalls that he was playing with the phone yesterday.

Sydney finishes the rest of her nightly cleaning ritual in thoughtful silence.

~

Carpious sits in darkness dozing off into unconsciousness. Ibuprofen was not strong enough to ease the throbbing in his left arm, so he took two muscle relaxers that were in his medicine cabinet from a back spasm he suffered last year. Exhaustion from not sleeping last night, coupled with the dulling effect of the medicine, lulls Carpious into a hollowed consciousness as he is slumped in a corner of his couch. His eyes are half closed and his mouth is agape while his head slowly leans to the side, losing its battle with gravity.

The sudden sound of the phone ringing jolts him awake, but his body is too drugged to completely spring into action. He stands, heavy with sleep, and stumbles around the couch looking for the phone that is deafening him with every ring. He returns to where he was sitting and finds the cordless phone on the floor.

"Hello?" he drawls.

"Hey, sweetie. Did I wake you?" Sydney asks on the other end.

Carpious massages his wounded and bandaged arm before falling back onto the couch. "No. I took some medicine and it's got me kind of drowsy and loopy, but

I wanted to hear your voice. How're you doing? I've missed you these past couple of days."

"I missed you too, sweetie. What's hurting you?"

Carpious looks down at his arm; it is illuminated by the glowing buttons on the phone. "I'm a little sore. Feverish and body aches. It feels like a bad cold or flu or something, but I can't slow down now. I have a flight in the morning. Fortunately, or unfortunately, it's a one-day trip."

"Oh, Carpious, I was going to say that I could come by and check on you in the morning after I dropped Solomon off. You sound like you need to stay home. Can't you cancel?"

"No, I'll be fine. I just need rest. I can take a couple of personal days when I get back. Besides, I wouldn't want you to get anything I have."

"Carpious, I'm a nurse. I'm around sick people all day long. Besides, I like the idea of taking care of you."

Sydney pauses as if she's waiting for Carpious to respond, but he says nothing. She continues, "Well, we'll have to spend some time together when you get back. I'm *so* sorry I missed your calls earlier. Solomon had turned the ringer off so I never heard the phone. Your voice sounded like something was wrong though. What's going on?"

"Hmmm…like I said, I was just missing you. I couldn't sleep last night after my sudden nap. I'm not sure what happened. I don't usually take naps."

"Your body was exhausted, and when we don't listen to our bodies, they shut down. I'm exhausted too. After I got Solomon settled in, I cleaned the kitchen and took a nice bath; and tomorrow, it's back to normal insanity.

Back to school and back to work. You missed a great message this morning at church."

"Yeah? What was it about?"

"Well, it made me think about our conversation the other day when you were over here and you showed me your release papers. My heart sank when I learned something I didn't know about you, something you didn't trust me with. But I thought about if that were me, if I had a secret that would cause someone to judge me—I'd probably be a bit apprehensive to share it as well. That's why I told you that there was no reason for me to forgive you. I love you and want our love to be open and honest. My marriage was built on a lie and I endured it. The events of today spoke to me because I was having second thoughts about accepting this new thing I learned about you. I was having doubts about forgiveness. I didn't want my words to just be saving face and being nice. And you know what, they aren't. I've searched my heart and I truly do accept you, Carpious. I want you to know that, and I don't want you to feel like you ever have to keep anything from me again."

Carpious straightens up from his drowsy disposition. "Thank you, Sydney. Thank you for loving me. I've always wanted acceptance, you know, even as a little kid—from my mom, from my dad...anyone. I've always wanted someone to want *me*. You're what I've always wanted, needed."

Carpious pauses and after a few moments, he continues. "Have you ever believed in something with such passion and conviction that you were willing to do anything to defend it, only to find out later that you were wrong?"

"Oh yeah, sure. I've jumped the gun on an assumption before. Who hasn't? Why?"

"What did that feel like to you? To find out that you were not only wrong but also perhaps humiliated at taking the stand that you did. Or even worse, did something irreversible while you were committed to that principle that no one else could possibly understand."

"I'm not sure. I would feel alone and confused, I suppose. Carpious, why? What did you do? What happened?"

"I didn't... I...Haleigh got hurt yesterday. She's fine now but her dad, Drew, was pretty upset because he didn't know her injuries were the result of an accident. And Lela—she's so fragile right now—I couldn't tell her about what happened. But..." Carpious inhales sharply. "It's Drew. He assumed that Haleigh's injuries were from another person hurting her and he flew into a rage. He ranted about what he was going to do to that person. I think he hurt that someone."

Carpious pauses. He continues with a tremble in his voice. "I think something bad has happened."

CHAPTER SIXTEEN

Ian Kaplan's body lies still on the floor of the kitchen of 361 Mechi Lane. He lies still because the life was strangled from him two days ago, because his muscle tissue remains in a contracted state until the proteins start to decompose.

Carpious left Ian just as he was when he died or, more specifically, was murdered, minus a few incriminating items. The barbecue fork that Carpious was stabbed with and the dishtowel he used to hide Ian's face while he strangled him are missing. Ian's gun has been wiped clean of any fingerprints and placed under the couch where it originally was before the confrontation.

The broken curio cabinet and accompanying glass strewn about the room has not moved, neither have the utensils and containers from the kitchen counter that surround Ian's corpse. A pool of clear liquid covers the floor where Ian lies, and the stinging smell indicates that it is household bleach, not water. The strong smell almost masks the stench of decaying flesh—almost. His pants are damp with bleach and the faded color on top indicates that it was poured over him.

Though Ian's eyes are still open, they are glassy and his pupils have turned a bluish gray. His mouth is slightly open and hosts a small swarm of gnats and flies that enter and exit at random. The side of his face stained with his own blood is now a dark red that looks almost black. His bare torso is pale-blue except for the large dark red spot where Carpious' knee was resting while he murdered him. A band of dark red and blue elongated bruises wraps around his neck like a scarf, a murderous memoir matching the contusion on his chest.

The outside temperature is only seventy-eight degrees, but the thermostat inside is set to ninety, an attempt to speed up the process of decomposition and to contaminate any remaining microscopic evidence. The television is still on and blaring.

Just outside Ian's home, a garbage truck squeals to a stop. A man in an orange jumpsuit drops off the back of the truck and grabs the metal trashcan and the giant rolling dumpster from the curb and empties the contents into the back end of the truck. A loud, whirring motor packs down the contents as the man in orange returns the trashcans to the curb.

~

A man wearing a loose fitting tie and white shirt peers over his horn-rimmed glasses at the woman on the other side of the counter. She is dressed in black pants and a white pressed shirt that is not tucked in. Her short hair is pulled back into a ponytail, but a few tufts are too short and stray from the others. She presses them back as she stands in front of the counter. A thick panel of plastic divides the two and there is a speaker in the center that hides the features of the woman who stands at five foot three. Underneath the speaker is a tray that dips into the counter. The man slides a clipboard to the other side and pushes a button to speak.

"Please read and sign here. I need to see some ID as well."

The woman reaches into her pocket and unfolds an envelope containing several pieces of paper and a driver's license that she slides across the tray to the other side. As she scribbles on the clipboard with the pen chained to the counter, the man studies the license and leans to the side to compare the features to the woman in front of him to the card. He returns her license to her as she slides the clipboard back to him.

"And who are you here to post bail for, Ms. Mightson?"

"Henderson. Asia Henderson."

The man's finger leads his eyes down a list of names in front of him as he frowns. He shakes his head.

"I don't see that name. Are you sure the judge set bail for her?"

"Um, yes, I'm sure."

"I have a Quintasia Henderson but no Asia Henderson."

"Yeah, that's her. My bad. I sometimes forget her full legal name since I've always called her Asia."

The man looks up at Alethea and sighs. "How do you want to pay for that? Check, money order, or credit card?"

"Money order. I have it right here. Two hundred fifty dollars, right?"

"That's right. Now you understand that Ms. Henderson must avoid any further trouble with the law and she can't leave the state before her court date or she will be arrested in contempt of court. *And* you will lose your money."

Alethea reaches into her envelope again. She places a pre-printed money order on the counter to fill in the blank that follows the words, "PAY TO THE ORDER OF."

"Yeah, I read that on the paper I just signed," she answers with a tone of sarcasm. "Who do I make this out to?"

The man points to a sign to Alethea's right that reads, "Make all checks money orders payable to MUNICIPAL COURT OF ADMAH CITY."

She fills in the blank and slides the money order across the tray. The man inspects it and turns it over to stamp it. "If you'll wait there, I'll process Ms. Henderson and release her to you shortly," he says as he points over Alethea's left shoulder.

She turns to see a small closet of a room that is furnished with four chairs and a coffee table that sits in the center of the room with ragged magazines on top.

She looks back to the man and asks, "How long?"

"The judge has to schedule her court date and she has a few papers to sign, so it should be about an hour."

Alethea scoffs and says, "Fine."

~

Fumes waft from the tailpipe of the blue, early model Civic as it idles at a red light. Alethea holds the shift in idle as it vibrates in tandem with the noisy rattle of the engine. On the passenger side sits Asia, a stocky woman with kinky hair that is pulled back into two full round puffs that sit atop the back of her head. She has her arms crossed as if in some private defiance.

"That motherfucka gone tell me that you can't leave town, like I can't read or somethin'. I swear, I was about to punch that cracker in the throat, girl," Alethea dramatically recalls, waving her left hand wildly.

Asia replies, "I know, girl. Folks be trippin'. This one bitch gonna roll up on me in there like she all up in my head and shit. It's a good thing you came when you did 'cause I was about to fuck her gay ass up."

The light changes to green as the car jerks into gear. A puff of smoke is forced from the back tailpipe as they sputter off.

"Girl, I feel you. You gotta go in that bitch like you crazy and nobody'll fuck wit' you. My bad that you was even there though. I don't know how you got caught up in any of this. You don't even use. Like what's that shit doing at your place all stashed like you some kinda dealer with a stash? But you know what, I got a feeling I know who did this."

Asia sits up wide-eyed and turns to face Alethea whose eyes are trained on the road.

"Who? You holdin' out on me? Who, Lee?"

Alethea glances at Asia.

"Girl, don't you even worry. I got this. You need to stay out of trouble anyway. Can I borrow your car for a couple of hours after I drop you off?"

"You don't even need to ask, Lee."

"I 'preciate it."

Asia settles back in her seat. "How you and that new dude doin'?"

"New dude? Who? Oh girl, he ain't 'bout shit. Nigga trippin' soon as I tell him I got the bug. He still want sex but he don't want no relationship, like I'm some kinda ho or somethin'."

"Girl, ain't *no* good men left out there. I ain't tryin' to sound like no dyke or nothin' but a sister gotta take care of herself or get a friend these days, you know what I'm sayin'?"

Alethea cuts her eyes at Asia. "I don't know 'bout you, but I need me a *man*. Some shit *I* can't do."

"That's what yo' friend is for."

"Shiiiiiit. You betta get out o' here with that shit."

The women laugh hysterically.

Asia sits back. "I see you wearing your job uniform. How they treatin' you?"

"It's all good. Just trying to stay positive and clean, you know, get my life right."

"I'm proud of you, girl. You go."

Alethea looks at Asia and smiles as she pulls the car into her driveway.

~

Alethea drops Asia off and makes her journey to Mechi Lane to confront Carpious about her suspicion, but because it's Wednesday during rush hour, the twenty-minute trip takes an hour and fifteen minutes. An already on-edge Alethea is now agitated and frustrated as well. She slows the car just before Carpious' house and parks alongside the curb, flicking a cigarette butt out of the blue Civic. She steps out and presses her hair back. A school bus has just dropped off a number of elementary-school-aged children that scatter to their homes; it pulls away and passes Alethea, who has started to walk up Carpious' driveway.

Parked in the driveway is an SUV belonging to Sydney who stopped by in hopes that she could surprise Carpious with an early dinner. Since he wasn't home yet, and she has a key, she decided to leave a note on his refrigerator that read:

Hi, sweetie. I stopped by to surprise you. I left dinner in the fridge for you. Enjoy, get some rest, and give me a call tonight. xoxo Sydney.

Alethea looks inside Sydney's vehicle as she walks past it to the front porch, when Sydney comes out of the front door.

"Oh, you startled me," she exclaims as she looks up to see Alethea standing at the foot of the stairs. "You're Alethea, right?"

Alethea glares up at her as Sydney reaches her hand out and introduces herself. "I'm Sydney."

Alethea reluctantly returns, "Yeah, we met before," while not extending her hand to receive Sydney's.

Sydney lets her hand fall to her side and scoffs as she continues down the steps past Alethea to the car. "Carpious is out of town so you'll have to *call* to tell him whatever it is that you need to tell him."

"He's not here? Where is he and why *you* coming out of *his* house like you live here too? Is ya'll like that?"

Sydney walks past Alethea but swings around, "You ask a lot of questions that don't concern you. Now I don't know what your business is with Carpious, but I can respect you enough to acknowledge that as *your* business. I expect the same respect. "

Alethea bristles and points a waving finger in Sydney's direction. "Look, bitch, don't be acting all uppity and shit. I know shit you can't even begin to think you know about yo' boyfriend."

Sydney turns to walk to her car. "I'm not even going to stoop to your level of immaturity, Alethea. I don't know what your problem is with me but I've done nothing to you to warrant your nasty attitude."

Sydney turns the key to unlock the car door but pauses short of getting in. She continues, "And don't think you can hold anything over me like you know some dark secret about Carpious that I don't. I know *everything*. We *share* everything."

On the other side of the vehicle, Alethea replies in a surprised tone shrugging her shoulders, "Really? Everything, huh? Like where he's been for the past twenty years? Like how and where we met?"

"Yes. *Really*. I *know* he was in prison for murder. I *know* that he met you online while he was incarcerated. I also *know* he left you after he found out you were an addict."

Alethea is quieted.

"Alethea, you seem like you've gotten yourself together. I'm not sure what your angle is or why you're coming back into Carpious' life, but you need to stand down. You need to stop calling and coming around uninvited. You need to just go."

Alethea comes around to the other side of the vehicle where Sydney is standing. "I was *minding* my own business until your boyfriend tried to have me sent back to jail. He gone and plant some drugs in my girl's place and called my probation officer like he was some concerned citizen next door, talking about people coming and going, buying drugs and shit. I hadn't even lived there in two months, so I *know* he lifted that address off o' some old shit."

"Carpious wouldn't do—"

"CARPIOUS WOULD! You think you know every-thing but you don't. *You* need to go...before he fucks *you* up too. My roommate got popped 'cause of some shit Carpious pulled. She don't even use, but her name is on the lease, now she got a court date. And I know it was him. The only way he could have got my girl's address was from the address he already had. But you know what? That shit gonna eventually blow back on him. He the same Carpious but got everybody fooled, including you."

Sydney gets in her car and starts the engine. "I don't have time for this, Alethea."

She begins backing out of the driveway and Alethea shouts, "Carpious *is* who he always *was*. Do you know who that is? Do you?"

Sydney's car disappears down the street leaving Alethea standing in Carpious' driveway alone.

~

There is no such anomaly as the perfect crime. There will always be an unknown variable, even with the most intricate conspiracies of murder or precise sciences of removing evidence from a crime scene.

Carpious is a man of detail and thought, despite his violent temper, which was unleashed on Ian four days ago resulting in death. He took great care in removing any fingerprints or traces of his own blood from the scene of his crime. He spent much thought in consider-ing what to cover up and what to leave for discovery in hopes of incriminating someone else. As a man whose career is spent pointing out the financial faults of others, he itemized all of the issues that would present themselves as liabilities in Ian's murder. But still, there is no such thing as the perfect crime.

A police car pulls into Ian's driveway and two officers step out. They approach the front door and one officer knocks and announces, "This is Officer Kemp with the Admah City Police. We need to speak with you for a moment."

No one answers.

His partner, Officer Warren, tries to look through the windows, but they are obscured by the drawn curtains. They wait a few more moments and walk around the side of the house to the back. Dogs are barking nearby and a few neighbors are standing on their porches and in their yards.

As the officers make their way to the back door, they see the broken glass on the panels. Kemp reaches for his transceiver while Warren puts his hand on his gun.

"This is 413. We have a 602 at 361 Mechi Lane. There was a report of a foul smell coming from this residence. We're confirming a broken glass entry and a foul smell coming from the back door of the residence. Please advise."

The transceiver beeps and a woman's voice drones, "Four-thirteen, proceed with caution."

The officers draw their weapons as Warren reaches in through the broken glass panel to unlock the door. He pushes the door open with his foot, but before they can both enter, the putrid odor of decaying flesh and heat greet them.

Warren looks at Kemp with a grimace on his face as they both step in and immediately see Ian's hardened body lying on the floor of the kitchen.

"I'll check the rest of the house," Warren says with his gun drawn as he continues past the kitchen.

Kemp carefully walks over to Ian's body and studies it before gingerly stepping back to the door. Warren returns, holstering his gun.

"All clear," he reports.

Kemp leads Warren outside and he makes a second call on the transceiver on his shoulder.

"We have a DB in decomp at 361 Mechi Lane that appears to be a homicide. Requesting an investigative unit immediately."

CHAPTER SEVENTEEN

Mechi Lane was a quiet little neighborhood before today. Now the whole neighborhood is a crime scene because of the murder of one Ian Kaplan at 361 Mechi Lane. The cul-de-sac is littered with police cars, and a large van, marked with the words MOBILE CRIME LAB, is parked in Ian's driveway. A vehicle that resembles an unmarked ambulance is parked backward behind it. Yellow police tape is strung around the perimeter of the lawn and dances in the breeze. More than a dozen curious neighbors have collected along the yellow boundary. They stand and wait like leeches waiting for the arrival of blood.

"Is he inside? No one has come out yet."

"I called the cops. I wonder if I'll get a reward."

"What happened?"

"Did he kill someone?"

"I heard they found another body."

"It was just a matter of time."

"I think he's on the run and they're searching for clues to find him."

As the gossip and chatter increase amidst the converging neighbors, a news van from Channel 2 pulls to a stop behind them. Two men spill out of the vehicle. One of those men is Frank Palmer, a handsome anchorman wearing a sport coat, slacks, and tie. The other man, Mike Shafer, is more casual, unkempt, and is toting a camera on his shoulder, holding a spool of cable and a microphone.

Frank walks past the crowd with an air of self-importance and is about to step over the police tape, just as a nearby uniformed officer approaches and says to him, "Sir, this area is under investigation. Can't you read? This is a crime scene."

"I was just trying to get your attention so that I could get a statement. I'm with Channel Two…"

"Sir, my supervisor will have a statement for you shortly, but you'll have to be patient until then so that we can do our job. Please step back."

Behind them, doors slam closed on an early model silver Cutlass that has parked just as crooked as the rest of the police vehicles. A dark-skinned woman in her forties with a short kinky afro and stocky build is accompanied by a tall, slender man with a potbelly and a slouched posture. His olive-toned skin gives off the appearance that he has just returned from somewhere sunny and would otherwise have a much pastier appearance. He has a professional-looking camera hanging around his neck. The couple walks up to the police boundary and the officer standing there lifts the tape upon seeing the woman's badge on her belt.

They duck under the tape and acknowledge the uniformed officer with a nod as they walk toward the house.

"Detectives," he verbally acknowledges.

Holding the microphone by his side, Frank turns to face the crowd he previously ignored that is now looking at him and the detectives who have just passed. Mike stands beside him with the camera on his shoulder not recording or trained on anyone.

"Does anyone here know what's going on? Did anyone see anything?" Frank asks.

~

Barbecue season is unofficially between the months of May and August in Admah City, and it's not unusual during that time to find many backyards littered with people holding disposable cups and plates and chattering over the most insignificant of concerns. Ian's backyard is filled with policemen but no one is holding cups filled with liquor or plates of food. The only seeming disposable thing present is Ian's body that still lies on his kitchen floor in a pool of bleach, waiting for the detectives to arrive to release the scene to the coroner who arrived well before them.

The nine police officers who have gathered on the scene might lead one to mistakenly think that there has been a mass homicide/suicide. The officers talk amongst themselves as the detectives, who have just arrived, reappear from around the side of the house.

"Who was the first one on the scene here?" the woman asks.

"I was," Kemp volunteers.

She nods politely. "I'm Detective Allen and this is my partner, Detective Ingalls. We need a statement from you and if you could walk us through what you saw when you got here…"

"No problem. My partner here, Warren, assisted me in securing the scene."

"We're going to need a statement from him too," Detective Ingalls speaks up.

"Okay."

As the officers lead the detectives to the back door, a man who was previously standing off by himself approaches. He's in his fifties and wearing glasses that are halfway down his nose and attire that a lawyer might wear on his day in court. His bald freckled head matches his face, which is also absent of any facial hair.

"When did the coroner start getting to the scene *before* the detectives?" he calls out as he approaches the detectives who are already crouched at the door looking at the broken glass.

Allen looks back over her shoulder at the coroner and stands to address him.

"Douche, we're sorry," Allen says with a smirk. "We're pulling double shifts and were working another case. We didn't see a need to put the lights on just to get over here. This DB isn't going anywhere. Besides, it's only been thirty minutes. You had all of these friendly patrolmen to keep you company."

"That's DeLouche and please respect *my* time, Detective Allen, or I'll start showing up late with your autopsy reports. Let's see you clear murders then."

Ingalls stands from inspecting the doorframe and broken glass pane. "Kids. Kids. Can't we all just get along here?" Ingalls smiles at his attempt at humor. "We're sorry, DeLouche. Okay? We're sorry we're late. Give us a few to take pictures of the scene and then we'll release the body to you. It shouldn't be too long. Okay?"

"Thank you," DeLouche says to Ingalls as he rolls his eyes at Allen.

The detectives follow Officer Kemp inside.

~

Detective Mahalia Allen is not popular for playing nice. As a woman of rank on the police force, she has had to be tougher than nails and harder working than most just to garner respect. On paper, her extensive education, references, an impressive list of endorsements by colleagues of stature speak well of her work. Though her last name may lead to the initial assumption that she is a Caucasian man, in real life, she's a stout black woman who stands at five foot two who forgot, somewhere along the way, that "playing nice" with the public was part of the game. Fortunately for her *and* her career, she's been partnered with Detective David Ingalls, a man who is much better at being in the right place at the right time than having any actual skill—but also, a man who has a way of getting his job done by being "nice" to people.

For three years, they have cleared case after case successfully, to the point that they are often placed on high-profile cases. When a man is killed in his own home in a middle-class neighborhood of influence in Admah City, it's a high-profile case.

Ian's body has been placed on a gurney in a white body bag and two officers are wheeling it out of the kitchen through the living room to the front door where the coroner's vehicle and several dozen curious neighbors now wait.

DeLouche is standing in the kitchen where Ian's body was, writing on a clipboard as Allen walks in. He pushes his glasses up from the tip of his nose and says to Allen, "I would put his time of death at about a week or so, but it's hard to tell because the temperature in here may have accelerated decomposition. I'll be able to tell more after the autopsy."

"What was the cause of death?" Allen asks.

"Well, he has several bruises and cuts on his face, arms, and torso which indicate that there was a struggle. He has a fractured hyoid and crushed trachea that is consistent with strangulation."

"Thank you, DeLouche," Ingalls chimes in ahead of Allen as she nods her head in affirmation.

"No problem," DeLouche replies as he leaves the kitchen.

~

Detective Allen and Ingalls are finishing their initial investigation of the scene as daylight fades. Only one police car remains outside 361 Mechi Lane.

Allen is enthusiastically talking through her theory of what happened with her partner who is trailing behind her.

"So our murderer breaks the glass pane on the back door for entry. This isn't brittle glass so it would have had to make a sound that *someone* outside had to hear."

Ingalls interrupts, "Maybe it was late and the immediate neighbors were asleep?"

"Possibly. We'll talk to the neighbors tomorrow to see what they know. There were no fibers on the edges of the broken glass, so the intruder may have wore some kind padded leather gloves that would have muffled the sound and protected his hands. He entered and walked to the living room where our victim was obviously watching television. The television was at a volume that may have masked the argument and struggle, making it unlikely that the neighbors heard anything out of the ordinary."

Ingalls walks around to the front of the couch and faces Allen. He adds, "The victim went for his weapon, which is when the struggle initiated. The intruder must have gotten the gun from him because the weapon was never discharged and…"

"No fingerprints are on the gun. There would have at least been the victim's prints on his own gun. The intruder wiped the gun clean. The struggle for the gun must have been here."

Allen walks over to the shattered curio cabinet.

"The victim must have gotten the best of his attacker at some point because he had time to drag himself into the kitchen as evidenced by the blood and glass from here and on his body…probably to retrieve the gun or some other weapon. There are also broken pieces of a vase so maybe he hit his attacker with it to distance himself."

Allen leads Ingalls into the kitchen.

She continues, "The struggle continued and the victim may have been going for another weapon when everything on the counter ended up on the floor. The attacker got the best of the victim here… but if everything fell off of the counter here, why are most of the articles all the way over there under the table?"

"The attacker was smart. He kicked anything that could have been used as a weapon away from him," Ingalls answers.

"He may have been smart, but unless he had eight arms, the victim must have gotten in at least one good shot. I think that he must have injured his attacker. That would explain the bleach. The attacker knew that if he contaminated the scene and the body with bleach that there'd be little chance we'd be able to distinguish his blood from the victim's."
"That makes sense. We should send all of the kitchen utensils to the lab for trace."

Allen frowns as she ponders in silence for a moment. "The victim *knew* his attacker. He had to. There is a gun that was *never* fired. If this were a simple robbery gone badly, the gun would have at least been discharged. And strangulation? That's almost always is a crime of passion where the attacker and the victim have some sort of relationship to one another. Yeah... these two knew each other."

~

Hours later, the activity and noise of the neighborhood have quieted. All of the vehicles that were previously parked in front of Ian's house are now gone. The police tape is the only remaining evidence that the safety of Mechi Lane has been violated.

Down the street in the comfort of his lair lies Carpious, like some lion after ingesting a gazelle. He's on his couch nestled between pillows, wearing only boxers and flipping through television channels. His attention is snatched abruptly and he sits up to see a familiar scene— his neighborhood on the 11 o'clock news.

A reporter from the television says:

"…spent Monday evening searching an Admah City neighborhood trying to piece together a homicide that left one man dead in his own home. Police declined to release the identity of the victim until his family could be notified, but his body was discovered this afternoon around 2 p.m. in a suburb north of the city.

"Admah City Police spokesman, Captain Patrick Hutton, said the investigation is ongoing and wouldn't comment regarding any leads.

"Neighbors are in shock.

"'I never thought anything like this could happen here. It's like a nightmare. Is anywhere safe?'

"One neighbor, who asked not to be identified, said she smelled a foul odor and called the police to complain, which led to their gruesome discovery.

"Some neighbors held hands and prayed as they awaited an update of what really happened.

"One resident said, 'We're praying for the man who was killed, praying for the neighborhood, and praying that they catch who did this before he hurts someone else. I've lived here for ten years and I thought we were safe here. I guess no one is immune to the evil that's out there these days. You just never know.'

"This is Frank Palmer for WKAC Channel 2, reporting live."

Carpious drags his massive hand over and down his face to his chin that is rich with stubble. He exhales deeply while turning the volume down on the television and tosses the remote to the other side of the couch as he falls backward into the oversized pillows staring at the ceiling. The phone suddenly rings. Carpious doesn't get up to answer it or to see who is calling. He just stares into space as if he can see beyond the ceiling. The lion will *not* sleep tonight.

CHAPTER EIGHTEEN

The dimness of a distant sound fails to disturb Carpious from the suspended consciousness that morning finds him in. He's spent several hours staring at the ceiling and pondering what he might do to escape suspicion if conjecture led the investigation his way.

The dampened sound of knocking from somewhere fails to arouse Carpious, who is asleep on his couch. Apparently, conspiring to get away with murder can be exhausting. Sundry thoughts have entangled his reason and rationale where the consideration of surrender is no more than an idea that was aborted soon after conception.

Hammering thuds in five-beat successions come from just outside Carpious' front door, but he barely stirs. Bernie, who is on the other end of the banging, determines that Carpious is either deep asleep or not home. He turns away from the door and returns across the street to resume observing his once-quiet neighborhood.

~

The ringing of a phone stabs into the black silence, startling Carpious awake. He jumps to his feet and fumbles to find the phone on an end table across from the couch. He picks it up on its final ring.

"Hello? Hello?"

No one answers.

He draws the phone from his ear to look at the display and sees that it was Sydney.

"Sydney? Was she just knocking?" he mumbles to himself as he shuffles to the front door.

He opens the door and light floods in, causing him to step back and squint. He sees Bernie trotting across the street to avoid the path of an oncoming blue Civic.

"Bernie?"

He steps out onto his porch a bit to look in the direction that Bernie is fixed on and he sees three uniformed policemen, along with a man and woman in regular dress who look like cops. They're making their way down the street, coming from the direction of Ian's house, talking to neighbors.

"Shit."

Carpious looks down at his phone again as he closes the door.

"How long was I sleep? Six missed calls?"

Six missed calls all from Sydney. Six attempts to reach Carpious since last night with no success.

Carpious walks back into the living room and picks up his watch from the coffee table. "Ten-seventeen."

He slips the watch onto his wrist and calls Sydney. The phone rings five times before going to voicemail. He doesn't leave a message. He calls again.

~

Before Ian was murdered, he sought to obtain as much information about Carpious as he could to prevent him from trying to bully him out of the neighborhood. In doing so, he learned of Alethea and arranged a face-to-face meeting with her. Ian was intuitive enough to glean information from her and her bitterness toward Carpious, and Alethea was more than willing to disclose everything she knew and experienced with her ex-husband—*after* Ian gave her $1,000.

Alethea's curiosity and her friend's blue Civic led her to visit Mechi Lane this morning. She slows past Carpious' house when she sees the police cars and activity. She barely notices Bernie crossing in front of her because she is so fixated on what's going on beyond him that sheds light on what she saw last night on the 11 o'clock news about someone who was killed in a quiet neighborhood that looked familiar to her. She was almost certain that it was a coincidence…until now. She continues to the end of the street to the cul-de-sac where Ian's house is.

An immensity of loneliness surrounding the house is punctuated by the amount of police tape that surrounds it. Alethea exclaims, "Motherfuck!"

She stops in front of the house and lingers there, staring as if she's waiting for Ian to come out the front door and say that everything is okay.

He doesn't.

Alethea continues slowly back up the street and pulls to park behind the police cars. The throaty clatter of the engine in idle draws the attention of the detectives who are talking to the residents at 229. Alethea turns the engine off and it issues a loud clanging disagreement before silencing. She gets out and walks toward the uniformed officers, but Detective Allen, who is already walking toward her, intercepts.

Allen approaches Alethea wearing a navy blue pant-suit and white blouse with her head cocked to the side, holding a small notebook and pen.

"May I help you?" she asks in an authoritative tone.

Alethea, who is dressed in gray sweatpants and a pink Minnie Mouse T-shirt, smoothes her frayed hair back with her fingers. She tucks a set of keys into a medium-sized leather purse that is dressier than her current ensemble.

"What happened?" Althea asks nodding toward Ian's house.

"Ma'am, who are you? Do you live here?"

Alethea looks around her before answering. "No."

"What is your business here then? This is a private community and we're conducting an investigation."

Alethea steps back, crossing her arms and making it more apparent that she's chewing gum. She appears annoyed at the questions as she looks at Detective Allen from head to toe. "I just wanted to know what was going on. That's all. Who you?"

"I'm Detective Allen and I'm investigating a *homicide* here. If you have no business here, I'm going to have to ask you to leave," she patiently asserts.

"Damn! You don't have to be so rude! If you *must* know, I *do* have business here. My ex-husband lives up the street *and* I know the man whose house is surrounded in yellow tape. I heard on the news that somethin' happened, that someone got killed."

Detective Allen sighs as she lifts her notebook in front of her with her pen ready to write. "What's your name, ma'am?"

Alethea looks at the notebook with a slight frown and then answers, "Alethea Mightson."

"And you say that your ex-husband lives in this community? Where?"

"He's at 163."

Alethea leans in to look at what Detective Allen is writing.

"How did you know the victim?" Detective Allen asks as she looks up from her notebook.

"Victim?"

"Ma'am, Mr. Kaplan is dead. Someone killed him. We're trying to find out who. Now how did you know him?"

"Who?"

"Ian Kaplan. The man who was killed?"

"Brunette dude? Nice teeth? I ain't into white dudes but he was kinda hot. *That* dude?"

"Yes. That man was killed in his home. We're investigating his murder."

Alethea's arrogant countenance changes and she stutters visibly shaken, "Oh, shit! Dead? Oh my god. Um…uh…"

Alethea stares at the ground, trying to collect her thoughts and recover from the shock of hearing what she'd already suspected. "I-I knew him through my ex-husband. They…they was in prison together."

Allen suddenly stops scribbling in her note-pad while trying to cloak her surprise. "Prison?"

"Uh…yeah. That's how…that's how they knew each other. My ex and Ian had a disagreement and Ian called me to see if I could convince him to change his mind."

"He called *you*?"

Alethea frowns as if the question is ridiculous. "Yeah."

"Why would Mr. Kaplan think that of all the reasonable choices of people to call to settle a dispute with your ex-husband, he would seek *you*, his neighbor's ex-wife? Most ex-wives don't have a lot of influence on their ex-husbands' decisions, so I'm not understanding how Mr. Kaplan thought that you might settle this *disagreement*."

"Look, all I know is he called me and I tried to contact my ex a couple of days ago but he was out of town."

"When was the last time you spoke to Mr. Kaplan?"

Alethea returns her eyes to the ground with a grimace of concentration on her face. "It was like last week, I think. Last…last Wednesday."

"And what was your ex-husband's offense?"

"Huh?"

"What did he do that landed him in jail?"

"Oh. Oh. He killed a dude."

Detective Allen rolls her eyes as she exhales and turns to see if her partner is in earshot. His attention is affixed on listening to a resident a few yards away. She whips back around to Alethea.

"What is your ex-husband's name, ma'am?"

"Carpious. Carpious Mightson."

~

Detective Ingalls has stopped writing down anything that forty-nine-year-old Dylan Hudson of 229 says. He's not talking about anything of value to their investigation, but he's been talking a long time. Ingalls listens as Dylan drones on.

"The dog up the street was barking up a storm the other night. That's unusual around here. I never heard that dog bark before that pedophile moved here. Somehow animals just know when people ain't right, you know. Animals got that sixth sense going."

The cell phone in Ingalls pocket vibrates giving him a legitimate reason and excuse to interrupt Dylan. He takes the phone out of his pocket and holds it up as evidence.

"Sorry, I have to take this."

He turns away from Dylan.

"Hello? Yeah? Right. Oh, that's great news. Okay. Are there any other techs there? Yeah. I understand. We'll be down shortly. Thanks."

Detective Ingalls slips the phone back in his pocket and calls out to Allen.

"Hey, after we get done with this next house, we need to go downtown. The lab says that that weapon tested positive on the double homicide and they may have a partial on this case that we need to run through the database."

"Can't the techs do that?"

"Not since the cases have backed up. We have to run our own prints now."

"Fine. We need to double back here afterward."

Ingalls turns back to Dylan.

"Thank you for your time, sir. You've been very helpful."

"No problem," Dylan returns.

~

Detective Ingalls walks across Lela Janson's lawn while his partner is trailing behind him still talking to Alethea.

"You take care of yourself and if you think of anything else, you call me," Detective Allen says in an almost motherly and uncharacteristic tone. She dips into her pocket and pulls out a business card and hands it to Alethea.

"Sure," Alethea answers with a rare smile. Alethea continues across the lawn toward Carpious' house; her smile fades.

Detective Allen joins Ingalls on the porch.

"Is she a lead?" Ingalls asks.

Allen is looking in Alethea's direction saying, "I'm not sure yet. There *is* something I want to check on when we get back to the precinct. You know, she reminds me of myself a little, when I was rough around the edges."

"When did you *stop* being rough around the edges?" Ingalls laughs and then knocks on the door. He steps back beside Allen and waits.

"Well, this is where all of our leads point."

"Not *all* of them," Allen mumbles.

Detective Ingalls looks confused by his partner's response. "What do you mean?"

But just at that moment, Lela opens the door. She's holding Caleb and Ingalls turns to smile at her.

"Good morning, ma'am. We're Detectives Ingalls and Allen with Admah City Police. We're investigating the murder of your neighbor, Ian Kaplan, and wanted to ask you and your husband some questions. Is your husband home?"

"No, he's not here."

Detective Allen joins in, "Is he at work? Can you tell us how to contact him?"

"I can give you his cell phone number," Lela volunteers as she bounces Caleb on her hip.

"Yes, we would appreciate that."

"A number of your neighbors said that your daughter was injured in front of Mr. Kaplan's home on Saturday. They said that she was very upset and your husband is known to have a bit of a temper from time to time."

"What? A *temper*? Who would say something like that?"

"A couple of your neighbors say that they have witnessed him having verbal outbursts with you and, in the past, other neighbors over trivial things."

Lela sighs as if she's yielding to defeat. "Drew can get angry but he's been under a lot of pressure lately with my pregnancy and work and…"

"Did your husband have a conversation with Mr. Kaplan after your daughter was injured?"

"No. It was my intention to talk to Mr. Kaplan to clear up a misunderstanding, but I've been so busy with this one here and my daughter that I haven't had the chance."

"Misunderstanding?"

"Yes. Apparently, Mr. Kaplan raised his voice at my daughter and she was upset by his tone. I didn't want him talking to my child or any of the children in the neighborhood that way."

"And your husband didn't have any contact with Mr. Kaplan since then?"

"Uhh, no. I…"

Detective Allen interjects from behind her partner, "Do you think your husband jumped to any conclusions, ma'am?"

"No. Drew is more logical than emotional. He would never hurt another person. I don't know anyone who is capable of what happened. That's horrible."

~

Meanwhile, a few homes away, a man quite capable of committing a crime is finally engaged in a conversation with Sydney.

"Are you *sure* you're okay?"

"Yes, love. I'm fine."

Sydney's voice crescendos, "Carpious, I tried calling you several times last night. I was so worried when I saw the news…"

"Baby, I know. I was knocked out last night. I didn't hear the phone at all."

"What happened? Why didn't you call *before* I was trying to call you?"

"Baby, I'm sorry. I got caught up in the excitement over here. It was crazy. There were police all over the place. We didn't know what was going on at first. I *just* looked outside and they're talking to a lot of the neighbors right now."

"Baby, you said something the other night about something bad happening. Do you think that this had anything to do with that?"

An abrupt and anxious knock on the door interrupts their conversation.

"Baby, I think the police are at the door. They must be about to question me now. I'll call you right back, okay?"

"Why are the pol—" Carpious ends the call before he can hear the rest of Sydney's question.

He returns the cordless phone to its base and walks to the door.

He inhales.

Then exhales and opens the door.

He looks down to see Alethea standing in front of him. She says, "You got about five minutes before the po po are standing here. Let me in now."

CHAPTER NINETEEN

Carpious stares back at Alethea as a stone wall might. His face gives no evidence of emotion, yet his presence echoes hints of danger. Alethea is defiant as she catches a glimpse of the Carpious she once knew.

"Let me in," she repeats as she pushes up against Carpious' unmoving frame.

He nudges her gently backward and growls through his teeth, "No. You need to leave and *never* darken my doorstep again."

"The police are coming down the street."

"And?"

"Yo' neighbor is dead. They questioning everybody to find out who killed him."

"And I will gladly answer whatever questions they have so that they find whoever did that horrible thing."

"Really, Carpious? I had my doubts but *that* answer, really? You better hope the cops don't see through you as easy as I do."

"What are you talking about?"

"Don't play stupid. Did you kill Ian? Did you kill yo' neighbor?"

Carpious' face flickers into a frown and he scoffs, "No. Why would you ask me something like that?"

"Um, hello, motherfucka. You done it before."

"You keep your voice *down*."

"Let me in then."

Carpious sighs heavily and steps aside for her to come inside. She takes a cigarette out of her purse and puts it between her lips as she struts past him swinging one of her arms by her side. Carpious stares in disbelief at her audacity before slamming the door behind her.

Alethea walks into the living room and plops down on the chair opposite of the couch. She lights the cigarette.

"Make yourself at home," Carpious sarcastically says waving his hands as he sits across from her.

Alethea takes a long drag on the cigarette and continues, "A few days ago, yo' neighbor got in touch with me. He wanted to talk all about you and how you was tryin' to blackmail him and shit. I'm not one to be in nobody else's drama. I'm tryin' to get *my* life together, you know what I'm sayin'? Anyhow, he started speaking my language when he offered me some money in exchange for talkin' 'bout you."

"About *me*?"

"Yeah. He wanted to know anything and everything about you. Like how we met and shit."

"And you *told* him?" Carpious feigns surprise as if he doesn't already know this.

"Hell yeah. A sistah got bills and *you* ain't tryin' to help. I told him everything I know, which is *everything*."

Carpious scoffs. "What does that mean? He already knows I was in prison. I have nothing to hide."

"Obviously you do. So, now he dead, Carpious. You kill 'im?"

A puff of smoke follows a short pause and Alethea answers her own question. "Yeah, you did it. You heartless motherfucka. You killed 'im. That ain't all I know 'bout neither. I know you tried to set me up. Got my girl in trouble and shit. You ain't slick, Carpious. I know all about your felonious ways. I made a mistake when I said we were alike. I ain't nothing like you."

Carpious calmly smiles and through his teeth he snarls, "You know… , you were always loud and never knew when to stop talking. You embarrass *yourself* and everyone around you. You are an uneducated, poverty-minded drug-fiend."

He stands and walks toward Alethea. Alethea takes another drag from her cigarette.

"You were something to look at once, but drugs and hard living have made you as ugly as your inside. You are an intolerable, insufferable hag. You don't know me. You don't know anything about what I'm capable of."

Alethea sarcastically claps. Ash from the end of the cigarette falls to the arm of the couch.

"Damnnnnn. You write that speech yourself or did your girlfriend help you with that?"

"You can't smoke in here, Alethea."

Carpious leans in and swings his massive hand across the front of Alethea's face, knocking the cigarette to the carpet. His fingertips glance her lips.

Alethea's eyes widen as she touches her mouth without looking at Carpious. She shakes her head vigorously back and forth as her expression returns to normal.

"Nah. You must think I'm stupid. I know what you tryin' to do. Nah, motherfucka! I ain't gettin' mixed up in yo' shit no mo'! I ain't goin' back to jail, but yo' ass is."

Alethea springs from the chair with the obvious intent on leaving, but Carpious grabs her by her arm and squeezes hard.

"You wanted to come in. *Stay* a while."

Carpious lets go of Alethea's arm as he slings her backward. She spins around, losing her balance, and falls into the chair. She stands up again, but Carpious is already blocking her path with his sheer size.

"Where're *you* going? You've been talking shit your whole life. Don't have any smart ass remarks now?"

He shoves her hard and she flips over the arm of the chair and falls into the table on the other side. Alethea flails as the phone and table fall to the ground with her.

She regains her composure and begins to get up as Carpious looms over her. She looks up at him with fear on her face as her voice trembles, "The police are just outside. You can't do this. I'll scream if you don't let me go now."

"Scream then!"

Alethea lets out the beginning of a scream right before Carpious reaches down and grabs her by the back of the neck, cutting off her ability to speak. He jerks her up with such force that he lets the momentum follow through and sits her down in the chair she was previously in.

He leans in over her and places a giant finger close to her face.

"I warned you to leave. I told you to leave but you kept coming back. You should have listened. You're no more than a loose end—a frayed strand that needs to be cut off an otherwise handsome suit."

Alethea realizes that the only way that she will walk out of the door at this point is to fight her way there. She looks Carpious in the eye and headbutts him. The sting and sudden surprise send him backward a few steps and he falls.

She springs up from the chair and leaps over Carpious who reaches out and grabs her by one of her legs. She falls and Carpious drags her toward him as he gets up.

Alethea frantically kicks into the air as if she's swimming to escape a shark who has detected the presence of her blood in the water.

She spins onto her back as Carpious drags her closer and sends a kick that rakes across his face.

First blood is drawn. Red races down his cheek.

Carpious grabs her free leg and covers them both with the weight of his own body as he advances toward her. He reaches for her neck and takes hold with one hand and squeezes.

Alethea digs her nails into his arm and draws more blood.

He squeezes tighter.

As her face becomes flush and she loses strength, she releases his arm and claws for his face or anything that will cause him to release his hold. She thrashes about trying fruitlessly to buck Carpious off of her but her arms are too short to reach anything of significance that may harm him and she is too small to budge a 220-pound man.

He squeezes tighter still.

Her protest weakens as she loses consciousness.

He continues to squeeze and stare into eyes that are starting to dim.

A knock at the door interrupts, as startling as thunder on a sunny day.

Carpious stops squeezing and looks up at the door. He looks back at Alethea who has gone limp.

"Shit!"

He chucks Alethea's body over his shoulder and carries her into the guestroom. As he passes the front door, he announces, "Just a minute!"

Carpious opens the closet in the guest room at the end of the hall. The closet is filled with several hanging coats and shirts while on the shelf are stacked boxes and blankets in no particular order. He drops Alethea into the corner on the floor and tosses a blanket on top of her. He snatches a long-sleeved, plaid shirt before closing the door to the closet and then the door to the bedroom.

Carpious stops by the bathroom and looks into the mirror to see his right arm covered in gouges and blood. He wipes the excess blood from his arm with a damp towel before putting on the shirt. As he quickly buttons the shirt, he looks at his reflection. The left side of his face is bloodied and skin has been loosened from his cheek. He dabs the blood and tries to affix the still attached skin back in place. He hears keys jangling in the front door.

"Sydney!"

~

Carpious' face flushes with fear and regret as he rushes to the front door.

"Sweetie, are you here?" Sydney calls out as she opens the door with Solomon trailing behind her.

Carpious reaches the door and opens it fully as Sydney is removing her key from the lock.

"Hey, love," he attempts to say in a chipper voice.

"Oh!" Sydney jumps back. "You startled me. I was worried."

As Carpious comes into full view, she sees his face.

"Oh my God, Carpious, what happened?"

"Alethea was here…"

"What? What happened? When? I just talked to you! Did you call the police?"

Carpious calmly responds, "Come in. Have a seat. I'll tell you about it. Hey, Solo."

"Hey," Solomon sheepishly replies when he see the blood on Carpious' face. Rather than bounding to Carpious with a hug, he continues to shadow his mother.

Carpious closes the door as Sydney and Solomon walk into the living room. Sydney sees the burn stain on the carpet from Alethea's cigarette and the overturned table.

"What happened in here? Oh my God. Solomon, go to the guest room so Carpious and I can talk. You can watch cartoons."

Carpious' eyes widen.

"Uh…he can stay in here."

"No, Carpious. I want to talk to you *alone*. He'll be fine. Come sit down and talk to me."

Carpious watches Solomon obediently walk down the hallway to the guest room and open the door. He exhales and sits on the couch beside Sydney.

Sydney touches his face gently and inspects his wound. He doesn't flinch. "This is going to need stitches."

Sydney sits back and looks intensely at Carpious who is frowning and looking away. "What's going on? You sounded so strange on the phone and now you look like this. I need you to be honest with me right now, Carpious. Talk to me."

Carpious closes his eyes and silently inhales.

Seconds pass while Carpious attempts to mouth words that find no ears. His eyes are still closed. Sydney sits in doting silence, waiting.

More seconds pass before Carpious exhales sharply and finally opens his eyes. Sydney leans in.

"My father took custody of me when my mother died of leukemia. I was twelve. Prior to that, I never really knew him as much as I knew *of* him. I grieved the loss of my mother, but I was elated to be in the custody of my ideological hero. One night, while I was sleeping, my father came into my bedroom. I was awakened by him removing my pajama bottoms. His weight and the putrid smell of alcohol and sweat overtook me. I couldn't move—either from fear or betrayal—I...he forced his penis inside me. And he didn't remove it until he ejaculated in me. I lay there, afterward, crying and covered in blood and semen."

Sydney whispers, "Oh my God..."

"He told me that this was how we would be connected as father and son forever, and it was our secret. He did it again and again until it no longer hurt me. I didn't feel *anything*. At all. One night, I found his gun and I aimed it at his face and pulled the trigger until it stopped firing. He didn't die, but that's why I went to jail in the first place. With that shame and injustice, my life changed forever. We *were* connected as father and son…forever. When an attempt was made in prison to rape me, I killed that man. I stabbed him to death, and when there was no life left in his body, I stabbed his soul to death. It wasn't self defense."

Carpious stops and closes his eyes again. The green and blue plaid sleeve that is covering his injured arm becomes dotted with blood. His breathing stutters loudly.

He opens his eyes and smacks his lips like he's parched from thirst. "The man who moved here last year, the sex offender, Ian Kaplan, we were connected *before* he moved here.

~

Detectives Allen and Ingalls walk past rows of soulless cubicles as they follow a hallway to a door marked CRIME LAB.

The white room is reminiscent of an empty morgue with the buzz of florescent lights overhead. Throughout the large room stand rows of high-standing tables with sinks and microscopes affixed to them. On the ends of the tables are stacked boxes filled with various sealed treasures that bring closure to some cases and more questions to others.

Allen immediately addresses a middle-aged woman seated near the door studying a computer screen.

"We got a call that you had something for us. Allen and Ingalls."

The woman looks up and nods and walks to one of the tables. She looks through several bags with red bands across the top of them and selects one. Attached to the bag is a sheet of paper that she removes and hands to the detectives.

Allen scans the printout and looks back up at the woman and smiles. "Thank you."

The woman nods back, never saying anything. The detectives turn to exit the lab and they walk two doors down into a room that is unmarked, much smaller, and dimly lit. Across the room are two monitors.

Allen, who has been leading Ingalls, steps back when they get to one of the monitors. "You go ahead," she says.

Ingalls smiles and sits down. "So why haven't you taken the class yet?"

Allen shrugs, "These computers. I don't know. I'm an old bird. As long as I have techy partners like you, I don't need to take a class."

Ingalls chuckles. "Somehow I feel like that's a shot at me and what I said a while ago about not needing to learn Spanish."

Allen leans over his shoulder as he enters his password and makes a few more keystrokes before coming to a screen where he reads silently.

"So, according to the lab tech, our database automatically flagged eleven possible matches for the partial recovered from one of the utensils on the scene."

"Let's have a look. I doubt that there's much to go on with a partial if our killer isn't in the system already. Innocent people aren't exactly lining up to submit their fingerprints for record."

"Sure they are. Whenever they apply for a driver's license. Wasn't there supposed to be a mandate a few years ago where the DMV has to file prints on license renewals?"

"Yeah, there was."

"Don't we have access to that? Wouldn't the data-base be populated with regular citizens to broaden our search?"

"It's on a completely different system that we don't yet have access to. Somewhere there sits a server with hundreds of thousands of scans that are useless to law enforcement. The wheels of bureaucracy roll slower than the wheels of justice in this town."

Ingalls cycles through the list of eleven names and their current addresses and a brief summary of their previous convictions.

"So far, none of these matches are in proximity to our victim. Wait. We have two. Jordan. He's incarcerated right now so he's unlikely. Mightson. This guy has been clean for—"

"Wait. Mightson? Pull him up."

Ingalls clicks on his name and the screen yields a photo and a detailed criminal history of Carpious—from the time that he was eighteen to the time that he was released from probation. Every insignificant detail is there, including his marital status and to whom he was married while he was on probation following his release.

"Look at the current address."

"Shit."

Allen claps her hands together.

"We have just cause to search his place and question him. My gut says that's our guy! Let's get the judge to sign off on a warrant and go pick Mr. Mightson up."

Ingalls spins around in the chair to face Allen who is already on her way out the door. "Wait. This guy has been clean for almost ten years. How can you be so sure?"

"Remember that woman wearing the Mickey Mouse shirt I was talking to earlier?"

"Yeah."

"That was his ex-wife. Her name's right there. We were one house away from talking to him. He and the victim were both in prison together. If Mightson has been clean all this time, maybe Kaplan was a threat somehow. Remember I said we needed to go back to that house?"

"Yeah."

"He's our man. Let's go!"

~

Down the hall from Carpious and Sydney and in the closet in the guest room where Solomon is watching TV, Alethea's body is crumpled in a corner on the floor and covered with a blanket. She's been left for dead until Carpious can dispose of her body and any evidence tying him to her murder.

The first problem with that line of rationale is Carpious, as her ex-husband, would be an instant suspect. Statistically, the husband, boyfriend, or ex is *always* a suspect and more than likely, the perpetrator.

The second problem with that line of rationale is that in order for there to be a crime to cover up, there has to be a *murder*.

The closet and its contents, which have been still and lifeless, suddenly shuffle in movement. Is it gravity settling the unbalanced weight of the blanket over Alethea's face? Or has life returned to the one who was left for dead?

Inanimate things may shift due to some unforeseen force, but only *living* things move of their own will.

The blanket slides from Alethea's face and her eyes open. Suddenly, she gasps for air.

CHAPTER TWENTY

Thirty-five years ago, Rhoda Mightson lay in a state of repose on the bed that had become her most likely place of occupation during her final days of a losing battle with leukemia. Her parents were no longer alive, nor did she have siblings to surround her bedside as she dispensed candies of wisdom and last words. The only one by her side was her world— Carpious.

She'd been quietly enduring her last days talking to Carpious until one day, Rhoda suffered respiratory failure.

She broke into a violent sweat and began convulsing and gasping for air. Carpious was horrified and he felt true fear and loss for the first time. As the hospice staff tried to revive her, all that Carpious could muster was, "Mommy, what's happening?"

Rhoda Mightson died that day.

~

In the guest room and oblivious to Carpious' confession, Solomon is sprawled across the bed on his stomach watching a cartoon DVD about robot spies who pose as humans. He's watched this cartoon dozens of times but is chuckling like it's his first.

Thump! A sound comes from the closet startling Solomon. Unsure if he's imagining things, he presses MUTE on the TV remote.

His eyes are wide as he listens.

Silence.

This time there is a shuffling sound before—Thump!

Solomon jumps from the bed and runs out of the room.

The closet doors swings open and Alethea unfolds onto the floor still gasping for air.

~

In the living room, Carpious is painfully continuing his confession to Sydney, "…blamed me, which is why she just started showing up again and again. Well, to-day…"

Solomon bursts into the room, "Mom!"

Sydney scolds, "Solomon Durden! *What* have I told you about interrupting?"

"But Mom, I heard something."

"Don't you see Carpious is talking?"

Solomon whines, "But Mom, I did—"

"Solomon! Over here."

Solomon obediently walks past Carpious and stands in front of his mom. Sydney takes Solomon firmly by both hands and looks him in the eyes.

"Mommy and Carpious are having a serious talk right now, sweetie. I need you to mind your manners and be quiet in the other room. Do you understand?"

In the guest room, Alethea manages to her feet. She scans the room before unplugging a glass lamp on the nightstand beside the bed. Hearing voices in the living room, she pads softly down the hallway holding the lamp above her head with the cord trailing behind her.

"Yes, ma'am," Solomon replies. "Mom?"

"Yes, Solomon."

"There's something in the closet. I heard it."

Solomon's words are like ice-cold water to Carpious' face and he tenses up. He is about to stand while looking at Sydney who looks at him and screams, "Carpious! No!"

Alethea is standing behind Carpious and she swings; a blur passes down toward him and comes to an abrupt and violent stop as it shatters on top of his head. Carpious falls to the ground like a marionette at the end of a performance.

Solomon whimpers, ""Mommy, what's happening?"

~

Sydney jumps to her feet to face Alethea while Solomon stands behind her clinging tightly to her waist. Carpious lies unconscious at her feet.

Alethea's chest heaves as she stands wavering like she's about to fall over. She looks down at Carpious and then up at Sydney who is staring back with a flash of disgust.

"H-he tried to kill me. He put his hands around my neck and tried to kill me. I never thought…"

Alethea grabs hold of the back of the sofa but her balance is too weak. She falls to her knees and begins to sob bitterly.

Sydney starts toward her but Solomon, who is wrapped tightly around her legs and waist, won't let her go or move with her. She looks down at him and sees him staring blankly at Carpious, his hero, on the ground. She kneels to block his view and embraces him tightly, looking away from it all.

A loud knock at the door startles the trio and a voice on the other side of the door asserts, "Open up. It's the police!"

~

Flashes of red and blue flicker across Sydney's face in broad daylight. She sits on the back bumper of her SUV holding Solomon close to her, shielding him from the ugliness of a beautiful, sunny day. Her cheeks are damp with tears as she quietly sniffles.

A few feet away, Detectives Allen and Ingalls are talking to Alethea who is sitting on the back of an ambulance. A paramedic has been attending to her while her statement is being taken. She has a neck brace on and a blanket draped over her back as her feet dangle off the edge of the ambulance. In between several dramatic re-enactments of what happened, Alethea breaks down crying. Ingalls sits beside her with one arm around her attempting to console her. Allen, who is not known for being as patient as her partner, leaves to get a statement from Sydney as well. As she walks up the driveway to where Sydney is sitting, two paramedics wheel a gurney carrying Carpious out the front door. He is strapped down and in a neck brace. The paramedics wheel him down the driveway and past Sydney and Allen to the second waiting ambulance on the street in front of the house. Sydney watches Carpious as he passes.

"Ms. Durden?" Detective Allen says as she approaches.

Sydney doesn't appear to hear or see Allen as her eyes are still trained on the gurney that is being lifted into the back of the ambulance.

"Ms. *Durden*," Allen says again with more emphasis as she steps into Sydney's field of view.

Sydney blinks back to consciousness but only to rise and follow the gurney, walking past Allen. Solomon is still clinging to her, making her long, deliberate strides somewhat awkward. As she nears the ambulance, she drags one hand across her face, wiping it of tears. Once she gets to the back of the vehicle, she looks in and sees Carpious. The gurney is raised about forty-five degrees and Carpious' eyes are open. He looks sedated and the top of his head is covered in gauze. A large bandage is over the left side of his face and partially obscures one of his eyes. His whole right arm is wrapped in bandages and crosses his torso to meet the other arm to which it is handcuffed.

Sydney stands there with Solomon clinging to her as she stares at the stranger of a man that she is—or was—in love with. She has always been the *strong* one. She has always been the last one standing. She has always been so...controlled.

But right now in her head, Sydney is crying and screaming and having a tantrum while asking, "Why? Why Carpious?"

But the words are not only in her head. They also escape her mouth. And more follow.

"Why, Carpious? Why? Why would you do this to *us*? Why would you lie about who you are and where you came from? Do *you* even know? Was this all some *con-man* game to you? Do you like playing with people lives, Carpious? Huh? *Do* you? Do you see this little boy, Carpious? He looked up to you. He loved you. *I* loved you. How could you do this, you bastard? And you hide behind God? God isn't in you. God doesn't *know* you. Nothing good will come to you, Carpious. You don't do people like this and walk free. You have to pay a price. And you will pay, Carpious. You will pay!"

Sydney's sobbing overcomes her words until they are no more than incoherent ramblings. Carpious' eyes are filled with regret but the neck brace wrapped tightly under his chin won't let him turn away from his shame, so he closes his eyes tightly.

"How could he?" Sydney whimpers as Detective Allen gently grasps her by the shoulders in an effort to calm her down. She directs Sydney away from the ambulance.

"Ms. Durden, I'm Detective Allen. I'm sorry that you and your son had to be involved in this, but I'm going to need a statement from you."

Sydney wipes her face and sniffles repeatedly.

"I would be happy to give you a *thorough* statement—starting from a year ago—about Carpious Mightson, or whoever he is."

Sydney looks down at Solomon who is hugging her tightly in silence. "I would prefer to come downtown and give you that statement tomorrow. This little guy has heard enough for today."

Detective Allen smiles and says, "I understand. That would be good. You get home and take care of yourself. We'll be in touch tomorrow."

~

"Ms. Mightson, do you need a ride home?" Detective Ingalls asks Alethea.

"Where is home?" she blankly replies.

"If you need, we can arrange to have your car taken to your residence and we can give you a ride. You're probably not in any condition to drive anyway."

Alethea stares past Ingalls into the emptiness of space.

"Ms. Mightson?" Ingalls repeats as he leans in to make contact with Alethea.

She slowly looks at him, drained and listless. "Where is home? I'm dying of a disease because nobody wanted me. Nobody wanted me so bad that he tried to kill me away. I can't even cry anymore. I got nothing. Yeah, take me home. Please. I don't know if I could find it on my own."

"Ms. Mightson, what you've been through today is going to take some time to sort through." He reaches into his pocket to pull out a wallet. He rifles through it and hands Alethea a card. "You can't do it alone. Give her a call. She's a really good listener who can help you sort through this."

Alethea takes the card and barely glances at it before saying, "Thanks."

~

MAN CHARGED WITH MURDER OF NEIGHBOR AND ATTEMPTED MURDER OF EX-WIFE

ADMAH CITY — He lived in a quiet, suburban community in north Admah City. He appeared to be an all-around, ordinary guy. He worked as a senior auditor for an investment firm and was a volunteer through an Admah City Community Church program, mentoring grade-school-aged boys. His lifestyle was simple and unassuming. Neighbors in the Mechi Lane community had no idea that Carpious Mightson was a previously convicted felon. He had served sixteen years of a twenty-year sentence for second-degree murder. "I'm still in shock," said Bernie Loomis, a neighbor and friend who lived right across the street from Mightson. "I never questioned him or where he came from because he led me to believe that he was formerly in the military and couldn't talk about stuff like that. I mean, I invited him into my home and drank good Scotch with this man. I am sick and disgusted that he could lie to all of us like this. Who can you trust these days?" Mightson allegedly strangled the victim, thirty-five-year-old Ian Kaplan, to death in his own home, but the two knew each other long before they were neighbors. Mightson served in the same prison and resided on the same cellblock as his victim and apparently there was animosity that had developed between them.

Last winter when Kaplan purchased a home at 361 Mechi Lane, many of his soon-to-be neighbors protested because Kaplan was a registered sex offender. One of the board members of the HOA, Amril Flores, said that she did all that she could to make him feel welcome and the rest of the neighborhood feel at peace.

"He was a quiet man and I got a sense that our children were safe. I sent a note to the homeowners and just cautioned them to be vigilant and watchful of their kids. I never could have imagined that this would happen."

Detective Mahalia Allen of the Admah City Fourth Precinct was the lead investigator on the case.

"If it wasn't for the hard work of our forensics team, we wouldn't have been able to bring solid evidence against Mr. Mightson and formally charge him. He was very careful, but not careful enough."

Mightson is also charged with the attempted murder of his ex-wife, Alethea Mightson. The woman was allegedly attacked by her ex-husband during a domestic dispute. When asked for comment, Ms. Mightson declined.

Though this is the first homicide that this neighborhood has seen in years, Admah City is no stranger to violent crime. Murders in the metro area jumped last year, up 12 percent from the previous year, according to statistics released by the FBI. Violent crimes, instigated by an increase in aggravated assaults, were up 4 percent. These crimes are steadily increasing as unemployment and foreclosure numbers continue to climb.

"I can't believe my little girl played in that guy's yard. You just *never* know who people are these days," said Drew Janson, Mightson's next-door neighbor.

Mightson will not be released on bond due to the violent nature of his crimes. He is scheduled to appear at a hearing to receive all formal charges next Tuesday.

~

It's been said that time heals all wounds, but the passage of time has little to do with healing and more to do with acceptance. The inhabitants of Mechi Lane have accepted the fact that their neighbor was not who he proclaimed to be. The ones who felt closest to him have welcomed the resentment that often comes shrink-wrapped with betrayal. Time will eventually offer them solace. If enough time passes, they may even find the will to forgive.

Four weeks have passed as Lela Janson sits on her porch cradling Caleb while she rocks back and forth on the swing. She's smiling as Caleb coos and gurgles. Mechi Lane has returned to some degree of normalcy as children play in their yards and neighbors carry on about their lives as if a murder and a murderer never happened.

Haleigh sits on the steps in front of Lela singing a tune she heard on the radio but doesn't know the words to. She's mimicking a dance with her doll .

Then, as random as seven-year-olds tend to be, she turns to her mother and says, "Mom, I miss Carpious. Where is he?"

Lela sighs as if she's answered this question many times before. "Honey, Carpious is gone to live in a different place now. He did something bad, so he has live there now."

"Jail?"

"Yes, sweetie. He's in jail."

Haleigh looks down and thoughtfully frowns while looking at her doll, which she's named Chloe.

She returns, "If Chloe did something bad, I would forgive her and still let her sleep in my bed. Why can't Carpious still live here if he says he's sorry?"

"Sweetie, sometimes saying you're sorry doesn't make the hurt go away that you caused other people. Sometimes, you need a time out. Carpious is in a time out."

"Oh. When is Daddy going to be come home? I miss him too."

Lela sighs as her previous smiles fades.

"Baby, Daddy is in a time out too, but it's different."

"He's in a different jail?"

"No, baby, he's not in jail. He did something that hurt Mommy, so he's living in a different house until he says that he's sorry."

"And *then* he can come home?"

Clouded thoughts of Drew and his whereabouts loom over Lela's head as she looks down at Caleb smiling. She revisits doubt over her decision to tell Drew to leave as she looks at the son who is already beginning to take on some of his father's physical characteristics.

She wonders, "How can I do this alone? I never wanted to be a single mother. I just *know* he was seeing some woman behind my back. But what if I was wrong? He was so defensive and closed off, but what if he really is innocent? Why won't he just tell me what's going on? How am I going to do this by myself?"

Lela is lost in her thoughts, unaware that Drew was *indeed* unfaithful to her and for a time, unfaithful to *himself*. Time and circumstance has since forced Drew to confront who he is and perhaps he will eventually confess that to Lela. Perhaps.

"Mommy?"

Lela's empty gaze is broken and she looks up at Haleigh. "Yes, baby?"

"And *then* he can come home?"

"I hope so, baby. We'll see. I'll give him a call to see if maybe he can stop by to kiss you good night before you go to sleep. How's that?"

Haleigh nods her head and resumes playing with her doll and singing the familiar song that she doesn't know the words to.

Lela sits back in the swing and resumes rocking back and forth while cradling Caleb.

CHAPTER TWENTY ONE

Carpious Mightson is who he's always been, but most of his life he's portrayed someone else. He wore the guise of a man of virtue and charisma while, all the while, he was a man of conflict and rage. People were drawn to him because he was handsome, appeared to be patient and wise, and reflected strength. All the while, he was repulsed by his own image in the mirror because he wasn't certain who was staring back at him. Carpious had become unsure as to which mask was really the true one.

Like every morning for the past sixteen months, Carpious begins his day on his knees as he prays silently. Fifteen years ago when he occupied a cell and was crouched on his knees in the same manner, it was more of a performance than a passion. But for about 475 days, Carpious has had no regard for what others think of him as he prays.

He rises from his knees and his massive frame dwarfs the eight-by-twelve-foot cell that he occupies alone. His bed consists of a pillow and a thin, flattened mattress that lies across a silver platform that is affixed to the wall. Beside his bed is a dull silver sink with a shelf above it. Atop the shelf are a thick spiral notebook, a weathered, dog-eared edition of a leather Bible with half the cover missing, a sliver of soap, and a pen. Bolted to the floor and less than two feet away is a stainless steel toilet.

Carpious reaches for his notebook and pen and sits on the bed. As he leafs through pages crisp with dried ink, he reflects on the words he's written over the past few months.

These days, and the passage of time, bring with them gifts of sobriety where once all that was there was chaos and punishment.

A lifetime ago, I sought something and someone I never knew. And I was overwhelmed with disappointment when that something and someone destroyed me. That is, it destroyed the child and innocence of Carpious Mightson.

Who was I then? Could that little boy uninterrupted have evolved into someone else—someone happy if my mother had not left me, had not died when she did. Would these words or this attempt at a journal exist? Perhaps I would have always longed for a father that I would never meet. I would've been better off—that's for certain. But maybe I would've always wondered what could've been…as I do now… but bloodless. Guiltless hands that don't leave behind fingerprints of condemnation and guilt.

But my hands and my mind are stained with actions and thoughts that only God can remove from me. I have tried to recreate my life with a new face while the inside was unchanged. I would see a reflec-

tion of me as if another was standing behind me and I couldn't see that other person…yet I was that other person all the while.

I have lived so much of my life in a muted count-down to rage. Three times of consequence, I have ex-acted that rage. Forty times of smaller incident, I have stammered and stumbled over my own smoldering anger. I and I alone have been my only devil.

Carpious closes his eyes and inhales silently as he takes in the words that he once wrote. He remembers the feeling that prompted such transparency. He recalls the day and the exact moment when he suddenly felt free to express himself, unfettered.

Carpious exhales after holding his breath with the recollection of thoughts. He looks out beyond his cell bars into space for a moment and smiles slightly before returning his attention to his notebook. He flips the pages ahead to another entry.

I am sorry. God forgive me. I'm sorry, Sydney. You are grace and forgiveness personified. I destroyed everything and you. I'm sorry for infecting Solomon with a memory that may very well be parallel to my own dim memories. While I never touched him in such a detestable manner as my father did me, I be-trayed him all the same.

I'm sorry, Mom. I took so much inside of me when you died. I hurt you so much when you were living… as if you didn't matter. I wanted a father who didn't want me. I wanted an ideal while making him an idol. And you were patient and strict and loving and pro-tective. You never prevented me from knowing my bastard of a father. You granted many opportunities for him to redeem himself as some kind of a father and a chance to be greater than the coward that you knew him to be. That coward never changed but you tried… even in death…you tried. I'm sorry, Mom. I love you.

Alethea, you always told the truth. Even in your rough-around-the-edges approach, you were true to who you are. I wanted different. Our marriage and relationship expired because I needed to be someone else. I needed to move forward and away from the monster that I felt I'd become. You thought you knew me, but you never knew what my father did to me. You never knew how I got caught up in the first place. You just accepted me as someone who wouldn't judge you for who you were. I could have been your savior but I needed to be saved. I'm sorry that my leaving led to your destruction. While I don't take responsibility for your lifestyle and its consequences, I do acknowledge the part I played in coldly cutting you off, in breaking your heart. I wasn't trying to break your heart.

Ian, I'm sorry I killed you. You were just as you said, but I didn't want to hear you. Your words angered me but told the truth at the same time. You and I were alike. But I was also right in saying that I was nothing like you. The difference between you and me at the time was that I was not at peace, as you were. A war was going on in me and you reflected all of the peace that I wanted. You also reflected my father and all of the hatred I wanted to spew at him but was never given the opportunity. Your past crime was like his against me. I didn't care so much about the little girl you sexually manipulated. In her place I saw me and my experiences. That's why I wanted you to go away. You were everything I hated about my past. I killed you but it wasn't personal. Not against you anyway. I'm sorry, Ian. I hope that God saw fit to have mercy on you. I hope that He has forgiven you for your crimes and that you are in heaven with him now.

Carpious frowns away a tear that accumulates in the corner of his eye before continuing to another page.

I was some kind of thespian portraying the champion. I would slay the dragons, kill the lurching beast, and allay the fears of the villagers. I would be celebrated as some kind of hero. And I would return to my lair, take off my armor, and bathe in a pool while my own reflection in the water would reveal the truth... I am not that champion...I am not a hero that the people honor. The blood on my armor and my sword doesn't belong to my enemies—it belongs to me.

I am the villain of the story.

Carpious continues to thumb through the notebook until he comes to a blank page. He reaches for the pen on the shelf and begins to write.

The Japanese poet Masahide once wrote, "The barn has burnt down—now I can see the moon." I now understand what that means. Life can truly begin after a fire when all is seemingly lost. All of the unnecessary has been burned away.

Carpious sits up and leans back against the wall as a controlled smile shines onto his face.

Suddenly a familiar buzz blares and drags into an echo, interrupting Carpious' thought. He turns to see his cell door slide open and the shadow of a guard. As per conditioned protocol, Carpious puts his notebook and pen to the side and stands, turns his back to the guard, and spreads his arms out to his side.

"RM13911, you have a visitor."

The guard takes Carpious' right arm and folds it behind his back as he places cuffs on his wrist and then does the same to his left. He turns him around to lead him out of the cell.

~

Carpious walks in silence down a long hallway through several doors that are buzzed open as the guard follows behind him. They come to an area that doesn't have the same cold, anesthetic feel that his current domicile does. Even the guards seem more human than the ones that he's become accustomed to interacting with. He passes a window that looks into a large room with several rows of tables and chairs. The room appears to be empty except for one person seated in the back.

Carpious stops at the door to the room, and the guard behind him removes the handcuffs.

"You have twenty minutes," the guard drones.

"Thank you," Carpious returns without turning to face him.

The door buzzes open as Carpious inhales.

Carpious enters the room and another guard is standing opposite of the door. He walks past him down the rows of tables. As he gets closer to the back of the room, he nervously reveals a hesitant smile.

Sydney, who is seated, smiles back. Carpious pulls out a chair and sits across from her.

"Hey," Carpious greets.

"Hi. You look like you've lost a little weight. Are you eating?"

"I am. You know, you don't have to keep…"

"Coming here?" Sydney interrupts.

"Yeah. I don't expect you…I mean you don't have to…"

"Yes I do. For *me*. I need closure to all of those feelings."

Carpious lowers his eyes to avoid Sydney's gentle glare.

"Well, I'm happy to see you all the same."

A few moments of silence pass.

Carpious resumes eye contact with Sydney.

"You look good. How's Solomon?"

"Thank you. He's good. His team finally won a game this past weekend."

Carpious' face brightens. "Really? That's good. That's really great."

"I think I may bring him next time. He keeps asking about you. He knows that I've been here."

Carpious leans against the back of his chair away from Sydney and his smile fades. "Really?"

"Yes, really. I think it's time."

Carpious looks down, suddenly ashamed. "Wow, Sydney. For three months you've been coming here and now…"

"Carpious, why is it *so* hard for you to accept grace? You keep waiting for the other shoe to drop. There *is* no other shoe. We've been over this. I'm not trying to make you feel guilty or punish you. *You* seem to be better at that than anyone anyway."

Carpious looks up and exhales sharply. He struggles to smile while leaning forward and fidgeting with his hands under the table. "I know, but I…"

Sydney stares back at Carpious saying nothing. Carpious fumbles on.

"I…Solomon is your son, and I know what I did tore everything apart. I know the look in his eyes that day. I had that same look when…"

Carpious chokes on silence.

"Your father molested you, Carpious. I know. You told me everything and…" Sydney closes her eyes and pauses for a moment collecting her thoughts. "While I don't agree with anything that you did, I understand why. As distorted and—excuse me—screwed up it is, I understand *why*. And *because* I understand, I can explain it to an eight-year-old who still loves you and *also* wants to understand."

Carpious struggles to smile as he continues to fidget. "Kids can be so forgiving, huh?"

"Yes, they can. And so can I. But can *you*? Can you forgive *yourself*, Carpious?"

"I'm working on it. I'm working on it. I've been journaling more, like you suggested. It's helping. To say things out loud and to see them written out on paper—it helps."

Carpious looks beyond Sydney, and stares into space for what feels like an eternity. She breaks the silence as if she's been telepathically cued.

"That's good. You keep doing that. It helped me a lot. I'm not sure that I could come here, let alone see your face, if I hadn't done the same thing. It helps to get all of your thoughts and feelings out on paper so that you can be honest with yourself. "

"You know, I ask God for grace and mercy and I've gotten both in so many ways. I know that what I did was terrible and I hurt a lot of people, but I can see God's grace and mercy now clearer than ever. And then you…you're the epitome of both in the flesh. You make me nervous, excited, ashamed, and thankful all at once. I can't say that I'm sorry enough. For destroying your world. For all that I did to hurt you."

Sydney smiles and Carpious looks away.

"How's that new guy treating you?"

"We're taking it slow. He's supportive of my visits here, so that's a good sign."

Carpious winces and smiles at Sydney. "Two words. Background check. I would hate for him to hurt you like I did."

Carpious' attempt at distracting himself from his discomfort fails as Sydney remains serious.

"Yes. You hurt me terribly, Carpious. You've also inadvertently taught me about myself. I love to think that I'm in control of my world in my bubble—my job, my son, my choices, and, once upon a time, you. The reality is I was *never* in control. God is. What I am learning is I can only control how I *respond* to whatever happens. I'm learning that I can forgive beyond just saying it and smiling. I'm learning that I can coexist with things that don't agree with *my way*. Speaking of such, I talked to Alethea a few days ago."

Carpious is surprised at the mere mention of Alethea's name.

"You did? Really?"

"Yes. She's still Alethea, but she's doing better. She doesn't feel the way that I do. You know, about moving forward. She has no desire to contact or even speak of you. She told me that I was stupid for visiting you once a month. She said that she did the same thing once and you left her after you got out of prison. I told her the difference is I'm not waiting on you. If you were to get out tomorrow, we would never be together the way we were before because the trust that I had is gone. But that doesn't mean that I don't love you."

Carpious nods quietly.

"Anyway, I ran into her because she started going to our church. I think Russell is helping her get plugged into some program that will take care of some of her medical expenses in exchange for her volunteer time with a teen addict support group in the city. She said she's still working, so I think she'll be okay."

"That's good to hear. That's really good. Russell is a good guy. He'll help her if she's willing. He came by a few months ago, but since the church has gotten so busy, he doesn't visit as often as he did.

"You sound…better. A couple of months ago, you sounded so dark. You alluded to suicidal resolutions. You were so abstract. I wasn't sure what to say to you so I just talked to the warden about my concerns."

Carpious laughs. "I know. You must've been *very* convincing. I was suddenly put on suicide watch for no reason. I had no idea why I was suddenly getting that kind of attention. I thought maybe I was unknowingly the target of some gang scuffle. And to be honest, I had no idea how dark my thoughts were becoming at the time. I was in a hole and unable to look up to know that I was in a dark place. I kept having dreams of Ian—kept seeing his face. I felt like I was going mad and all I could think about was making the noise stop."

"Well, I'm glad you got what you needed."

"I have my days, but for the most part I feel...healed. I'm in a better place now. I can finally be *me*, you know? For once in my life I can accept who I am. Sydney, that man who hurt you and did all of those horrible things, that wasn't me. I mean it *was* me in the flesh and I take responsibility for that, but it wasn't the *real* me. I became this figment of my own doing. I was daydreaming, knowing that I would eventually have to wake up. I was chasing a speeding car that was going to eventually to stop. But you know, all that happened with us, that was real. My feelings for you were the only thing that was real."

Tears rush from Carpious' eyes while he puts his hands on the table in front of Sydney. He doesn't attempt to brush the tears away or turn his face to hide them. Instead he reaches out both of his upturned and open palms as a surrendering gesture for her hands. She extends her hands and rests them on top of his. He clasps her fingers gently, looking into her eyes and smiles.

"Sydney, thank you," Carpious exhales.

Composed and receptive, Sydney smiles back, "You're welcome."

~

Carpious Mightson is who he's always been, but once, he wore the guise of Pious Almighty. Holier than thou. The Prince of Pride. And the King of Condescension. Once, he was not who he appeared to be while portraying all that he wanted to be.

But that was a long time ago. Carpious has since been stripped of the pride that would prevent him from seeing his own crimes. He's been stripped of the facade that he brandished to mask his own sins. He's been stripped of the garments that only made him more ashamed when he saw his reflection. He's been stripped down to a mere man. A man he has forgiven.

About the Author

Kenn Bivins Kenn was born in Macon, Georgia in 1970. He worked as a layout artist and painter before evolving into a freelance illustrator who worked in many mediums that included comic books, magazines, and animation. Eventually his reach evolved into interactive media, developing websites and online animation.

Presently, Kenn works at an advertising agency as an Art Director, overseeing design and execution of websites and applications. Even though his background is layered in the arts, Kenn has always been a writer.

He states, "Even if I'm simply illustrating a cat, there is a story in my head about that cat – how he moves, why his tail is so bushy, whether he sleeps on a windowsill or under a bed, and so on. Words aren't the only means to tell a story. I like to think of myself as a modern day griot. A griot is a member of a certain social distinction in western Africa whose primary function is to keep an oral history of the tribe or the village. This person would use song, dance, poems, or whatever to do so. Parallel to that, I use pictures, words, code, or whatever tools necessary to articulate my own narrative.

Kenn currently lives in Atlanta, Georgia with his two sons. He is already at work, writing his next exciting tale. PIOUS is his first novel.

Acknowledgements

To my Dad and the God of the creation – Thank you for second chances.

To Mom – Thank you for your sacrifice.

To Aaron Alon, Samara Barks, Yolanda Cooper, Shenell Dawson, Lara Falberg, Heather Alon Friedman, Miranda Madar, Marura Lenjo, Tonya Parker, Toriana Mikielle Smith, Lyn Thomas, James Tomasino, and DeVeata Williams – I owe a tremendous degree of gratitude to you for your edits, critiques, advice, and encouragement while *PIOUS* was being crafted. It would not be what it has become without your support. And if there are any misspelled words, it's all your fault.

To those random and unsuspecting strangers who inspired some of the characters within – Be careful what you do. You're being watched.

To Bear McCreary, Ben Harper, Calexico, Nina Simone, and Switchfoot – I constantly reach to write like your melody.

Now that you've read *PIOUS*, visit www.piousbook.com for bonus material and to join the conversation about the book.